LADY ILENA

Way of the Warrior

Patricia Malone

Published by Laurel-Leaf
an imprint of Random House Children's Books
a division of Random House, Inc.
New York

This is a work of fiction. Names, characters, places, and incidents either are
the product of the author's imagination or are used fictitiously. Any resemblance
to actual persons, living or dead, events, or locales is entirely coincidental.

Originally published in hardcover in the United States by Delacorte Press, New
York, in 2005. This edition published by arrangement with Delacorte Press.

Laurel-Leaf and colophon are registered trademarks of Random House, Inc.

www.randomhouse.com/teens

Educators and librarians, for a variety of teaching tools, visit us at
www.randomhouse.com/teachers

RL: 5.1
ISBN: 978-0-440-23901-7
August 2007
Printed in the United States of America

10 9 8 7 6 5 4 3 2 1

First Laurel-Leaf Edition

LADY ILENA

Way of the Warrior

Inset:
River Leven
Cameliard
Alcluith
River Clota

Dun Lachan
Dun Dreug
River Dee
Dun Struan
Vale of Enfert
Dun Alyn

NORTH SEA

See Inset

ERIU

Gorre
Uxelodunum

IRISH SEA

SAXON TERRITORY

London

ATLANTIC OCEAN

BRITAIN
A.D. 500

0   50   100   150
Scale of Miles

N
W   E
S

Chapter 1

"Must you leave tomorrow?" I ask.

Durant and I sit, wrapped warmly in his traveling cloak, watching the hearth fire flicker and talking of our plans for the future. Wind howls outside the fortress while the rough sea attacks the cliffs below us. My head is snug against his shoulder, and I can feel his chest move as he sighs.

"You know I don't want to go, Ilena," he says, "but Hoel and I have lingered ten days past the time that we planned, and winter weather makes traveling through the mountains more dangerous every day. Arthur expects us."

I know that, of course. Saxons have been settling in the South of Britain for years, but now they come into the North, and some fortresses here welcome them. Arthur, also

1

known as the Dragon Chief, is building an alliance to keep Saxons out of our northern territory. Durant and his friend Hoel are his most trusted lieutenants, and the information they have for him is important.

"I am glad that you have stayed this long," I say.

He laughs. "Yes, and I have an extra piece of news for Arthur because of it."

We intended to wait until Durant returned in the spring to announce our marriage plans, but my father, Belert, urged us to consider the matter immediately.

Hoel agreed. "What better way to make Dun Alyn's alliance with Arthur clear than to announce a betrothal between Durant of Arthur's table and Ilena, chief of Dun Alyn?"

"Let the bards spread the news throughout the winter," Belert said. Then he grinned and added, "And I'll be spared the nuisance of suitors swarming at our gates asking for my beautiful daughter."

Despite my father's bantering tone, his announcement of our betrothal at the banquet earlier tonight made it clear how pleased he is with our plans. "Durant of Hadel is a great warrior. He rides at Arthur's right hand, and bards throughout the land sing of his courage and wisdom. He and Ilena will wed in the spring and rule Dun Alyn well."

We ended the evening with the Great Oath. Durant's arm was warm against mine as we stood together, and our voices blended as we spoke.

"Heaven is above us, and the earth is beneath us, and

2

the sea is round about us. Unless the sky shall fall with its showers of stars on the ground, or unless the earth be rent apart, or unless the waves of the blue sea come over the forests of the living world, we will stand with Arthur."

Those ancient words bind all of us to follow Arthur whenever he calls us. We are sworn to protect him at all costs and to give up our own lives to keep him from harm. The people of Dun Alyn swore that oath to me on the night that I was recognized as hereditary chief, and then I joined with them as we pledged ourselves to Belert. This has been the custom of our people for generations and generations, and it accounts for our strength in battle. Our honor as individuals depends on our courage and our loyalty to those we swear to protect.

"It is late," I say. "You need sleep if you are to get an early start tomorrow." I make myself move away from him.

Durant leans forward and stirs the fire. The flames blaze up and light his face for a few moments, and I try to memorize every detail. His fair complexion is flushed from the fire, and his auburn hair falls around his face, blending with his short beard. His eyes look gray in the firelight though I know that flecks of green appear in daylight. He is tall, with the broad muscular build of a warrior.

When he turns back to me, he says, "I can hardly bear to leave you, Ilena. I'll think of you every day that we are apart."

"And I of you," I respond. I dread the long snowy months until he returns.

3

"You will be busy," he says. "You've a fortress to govern."

"Belert does that," I say.

"You are the hereditary chief, Ilena." Durant's voice is firm. "People expect leadership from you."

I struggle to make sense of this. I have trained all my life as a warrior, absorbed the lessons of loyalty, courage, and self-sacrifice, but I never thought of myself as a chief until I came to Dun Alyn. "I will depend on my father's counsel until you come to rule beside me," I say.

He shakes his head. "I will not always be beside you. I owe allegiance to Arthur and will often be away on his business. A true chief must be strong and able to stand alone when it is necessary."

"But you will come as soon as possible in the spring?"

"Aye. As soon as the snows melt in the high passes." He reaches out to hold me close again.

We stay beside the hearth until the last coals grow dim and thick with ash.

✳ ✳ ✳

The northeast wind continues through the night and by morning is throwing icy blasts of rain across the fortress grounds. Durant, Hoel, and their three companions are at the gate as soon as dawn lightens the cloudy sky. I've gathered food for their packs and seen that their waterskins are full.

"At least the wind will be at our backs," Hoel grumbles, "though this time of year it can shift fast enough."

"It might let up as we leave the coast," Durant says. "Go on; I'll follow you in a moment." We stand close together beside his big gray stallion and watch the others ride out through the gate. As is the custom on entering or leaving a fortress, Hoel has raised a standard, the red and white dragon pennant of Arthur's troops, and it whips above their heads as they move back and forth through the maze of earthen walls that secures the approach to Dun Alyn.

Durant pulls a chain with a gold ring on it from around his neck.

"I have no fine gift for you or for your father. I will bring both when I come, but wear this until then." He puts it over my head, lifting my hair gently out of the way.

I hold the ring so that I can study it. The thick yellow metal is carved with branches and leaves. The oval mount is rimmed with a gold rope design and holds a sculpted stone that is layered in different shades of deep blue-red. Two horses carved into the stone stand out against darker red layers around them.

"I've never seen you without this," I say. "It is beautiful." The horses blur as my eyes fill with tears. I wonder how often I'll stare at them and think of Durant before he returns to me. I drop the ring inside my tunic and wipe my eyes with the edge of my cloak.

"It was given to my great-great-grandfather by the

Roman Duke of War himself," he says. "Someday it will belong to my son."

He has told me about Aidan, who is five years old, and has also talked of the child's mother, who died when Aidan was born. We plan to travel to Durant's home fortress of Hadel after our wedding and bring the boy back to live with us here.

We hold each other for what seems a very short time; when he loosens his arms, I cling tightly for another moment, then step back to let him go. Once on horseback, he removes his war helmet from its hook on the saddle and pulls it on. I reach up to grasp his hand one more time.

"Until spring," I say.

He nods. "Until spring. God keep you safe for me."

"And may he guard you while we are apart." I watch as he moves through the gate, then hurry to the ladder that leads to the walltop.

By the time I've climbed onto the ramparts, Durant has cleared the defensive ring and is on his way down the steep road to the spot where Hoel and the others are waiting. I watch, clutching my cloak tight against the rain, as the five of them, Hoel and Durant in the lead, the horses at a canter, and the long dragon pennant snapping in the wind above their heads, proceed along the trail that leads into the forest. When they reach tree cover, the group stops; Hoel furls the pennant around the spear that holds it, and Durant turns to look back toward Dun Alyn.

I wave and he raises his hand in response, then follows his companions onto the path that leads through the woods to the mountains.

I hurry to my room, thankful for the rain against my face because it hides the tears I can't keep back.

Only three of us live in the family quarters. Belert's large room is next to mine. Spusscio, my father's friend and advisor, lives in a room across the central hearth area.

My room belonged to my sister, Miquain, who died last summer in battle. Belert has made it plain that everything here is now mine, and the clothes that I brought from the Vale of Enfert are mixed with hers in the larchwood storage boxes. My cloak hangs on a peg by the door, and my sword and shield have their place in the corner. I stir the small fire into a blaze and fasten the window shutters more tightly against the wind, then fall onto the bedplace and bury my face in the soft furs that cover it.

The long winter stretches ahead without Durant. I've a new life, new tasks, but suddenly I'm homesick for my old house in the Vale of Enfert, for my dog, Cryner, for my friends there, and most of all for my parents—my foster parents—whose graves lie high above that valley.

"Ilena?" It's Spusscio.

I swipe a bedskin across my face before I answer. "Come in."

He opens the wicker door, and a young hound pushes past him and leaps up beside me. A rough tongue rakes my face, taking care of any remaining tears, and his tail whips my arm as he clambers across me. I smile in spite of my sorrow.

"Down, Machonna!" Spusscio commands. "Ilena won't like you if you have no manners!" Spusscio is a dwarf; the top of his head does not reach my shoulder. His voice, however, is as gruff as any man's, and his authority as my father's closest confidant is rarely questioned.

The dog takes one last sniff of the bedskins, leaps to the floor, and, eyeing the fire with some concern, circles back to Spusscio's side. He sits with his left ear up and his right one drooping down, his dark eyes scanning the room, and his tail swishing softly on the stone floor. The ear that folds over is a light red-brown, and the color strays down onto his face to surround his right eye; the rest of his face and body is white.

"The old superstition!" I say. A white animal is thought by many to come from the other world, and a red mark is especially alarming to people who fear spirits. "I'm surprised that he has survived."

"Aye. Everyone knows they'll answer to me if anything happens to him, but he could use another friend in the fortress." He looks down at the dog. "Would you like to stay with the lady, Machonna?"

"I'd love his company; I miss my old hound. Come, boy."

Spusscio points to me. "It's all right. Stay with Ilena."

Machonna leaps back up beside me and starts to lick.

8

When Spusscio gets to the door, the dog looks toward him, then back at me.

"Hold his collar while I leave. He'll be fine." He watches the two of us for a moment before adding, "I've told your weapons class to meet in the Great Hall at half noon."

Teaching the young warriors of Dun Alyn will be one of my main tasks. While Durant and his companions were here, we held several sessions of games and weapons demonstrations with all our warriors, the young and the experienced, taking part. Now it is time to start regular training sessions that will go on throughout the winter.

"Good," I say. "It is time to get to work."

Machonna watches Spusscio leave, then stretches out on my bedplace and dozes as I twist my hair into a braid and change into trousers and battle vest. When I've gathered my sword and shield from their corner, he prances beside me on our way to the Great Hall.

Tables have been dismantled to clear space for us, and six young people mill around the fire. Talking ceases when I enter, and all turn to stare at me. I'm not sure how to begin, so I stand still and smile while I think about what to say.

"Are you all here?" Spusscio's voice booms from the doorway behind me. "Where's Sorcha?"

No one speaks.

Spusscio stomps across the room, grumbling as he goes. "I said midmorning. It's well past that."

"I've been grieving for my grandfather." The shrill voice comes from the doorway and sets my teeth on edge.

"Welcome, Sorcha," Spusscio says. "Come and take a seat. I want to talk about the things that have happened at Dun Alyn."

I would not have known who she was if he hadn't said her name. When I spoke with her on the day after her grandfather's death, I thought she was a child. She kept her head down, and her hair had fallen across her face, partially hiding her tear-swollen eyes. She ran from me that day and has kept out of my sight since then.

Now I see that Sorcha is no child. She is not much taller than Spusscio, but her hair is plaited off of her face, her shoulders are back so that her breasts shape the tunic beneath her war vest, her chin is high, and her eyes are blazing. She strides across the room and stops for a moment, surveying the others, then glares at me and sits as far from me as possible.

When she speaks again her voice is a little quieter, but it is still far different from the hesitant tone I remember. This is a young woman—one who seems to change her appearance as she chooses. "Then tell the truth about what happened, Spusscio. Ilena killed my grandfather!"

Her words tear through me like a knife. I feel as if I'm back on the walltop, clinging with one arm to the rough rock ledge while her grandfather, Ogern, dangled for a painful few moments from my other arm before losing his grip and dropping to the rocks far below.

"Your grandfather tried to kill Ilena," Spusscio says.

"She pushed him off the wall," Sorcha says. Her voice is shrill again.

"Ogern tried to push Ilena off the walltop, but he lost his balance and both of them fell. Ilena managed to hang on, but he did not." Spusscio looks at each of the young people in turn. "Are there any questions?" He turns to Sorcha last and holds his gaze on her face.

Sorcha's voice is flat now, without emotion. "Very well. That is the story you tell. My grandfather—Druid of Dun Alyn and uncle of Chief Cara—is dead. I, who have lived at Dun Alyn all my life, must give up my claim as chief because some unknown person"—she turns to look at me for a long silent moment—"who had never been in this fortress, who was raised among strangers, with no knowledge of our customs, has wandered into our Great Hall and claimed to be Belert's daughter."

"And so she is, and more important, she is Cara's firstborn daughter and thus became the rightful chief at Cara's death." He looks around the group for a few moments before he continues.

"Let us go back farther—to Dun Alyn's darkest hour. That hot summer day three months ago. You were with us on the hunt, Sorcha—and you, Rory." He nods to a tall

11

young man on the back bench. "Some of you were in the high meadow with the cattle, others going about your work in the fortress. I'll wager none of you will ever forget what you were doing when the horns sounded."

They shift in place and shake their heads. Even Sorcha sits quietly as she remembers. Spusscio's voice is softer now but easily heard in the silent hall.

"A raid. With no warning. Strangers at our gate—Saxons among them but others from here in the North also. I've not yet learned the fortresses they came from."

"We tried to get back," Rory says.

"Yes," Spusscio says, "we tried. When we heard the horns, we raced, Belert in the lead, as hard as we could push the horses. But it was too late. Our beloved Chief Cara and her daughter Miquain were dead when we arrived. None of the raiders escaped our swords, but that was little comfort to us."

Sorcha says, "And my grandfather told me that I was the new chief. Cara and my mother were cousins."

Spusscio says, "Yes, as far as we knew at the time, Sorcha was the heir to Dun Alyn. But you've all heard the story; you were in the hall the night Ilena was brought in. Some pretended to think she was a spirit, but when her background was pieced together, we knew she was the true chief of Dun Alyn. She is the daughter of Cara, twin sister to Miquain. Because of the superstition about twins, Cara had to send Ilena away. Moren, Cara's brother, and his wife, Grenna, carried Ilena to safety in the West."

Sorcha says something so quietly that I can't hear it.

Spusscio shakes his head and looks at the group. "Ilena is your chief! You will meet each day at midmorning for weapons practice unless she makes other plans for you."

I stand and speak with what I hope is an air of authority. "Does everyone have sword and shield?"

"Yes, lady," Rory says. "We've all brought our own."

"You did well in the skirmishes, Rory," I say. In one of the mock sword fights yesterday, he held his own against Durant for some time before his sword flew from his hand and he had to kneel in defeat.

He looks pleased. "Thank you."

I look at the others. "All of you took part at one time or another; I watched you closely, and I am impressed with your ability." I'm careful not to look at Sorcha.

"I did not participate in games with men from Arthur's troop," she says. "I would have been tempted to harm one of them."

I turn to meet her gaze with as much dignity as I can muster. I understand her grief and her anger at me, but I am chief of Dun Alyn—by birth, by training, by law—and I will not appear weak before her. "I have not seen you work with sword or spear, but I doubt that you could have bested any one of the five," I say. "And remember that Durant will be chief beside me; you will see Arthur's people in Dun Alyn often."

She stands and picks up her shield and sword. "If I am here."

"And where would you be?" Spusscio snaps.

"I'm leaving tomorrow to visit our relatives at Dun Struan," she says.

A flash of anger crosses his face, but his voice is level. "When was that decided?"

"I've talked to Belert. You don't know everything that happens in this fortress." She stalks to the door and turns back to glare at me. "We'll see what the rest of our family thinks of this stranger pushing me out of my home and my position."

I can feel the tension in the room ease as she leaves. My other students shift on their benches, look at each other, then focus on me. I take a deep breath and try to sound matter-of-fact.

"Let's get started," I say.

Spusscio snaps his fingers at Machonna and stomps to the far end of the hall with the dog close behind him.

I set my pupils to work on exercises in strength training and watch closely to see who might need a different sword or additional practice with a heavy iron bar. When they are tired, I urge them on for a few more swings and lunges, then tell them to rest.

Spusscio has been watching while Machonna has napped on the straw behind him. I wander back to them while my students relax.

"They are well trained already," I say.

"Aye," he says. "Cara—your mother—was a skilled teacher. As you are."

"Thank you," I reply, pleased at the compliment. "I am simply doing what Moren did as he taught me."

"I didn't know Moren, but Cara and Belert spoke of him often. He was said to be the best war leader and teacher in Britain. His absence was a great loss for Dun Alyn."

It is hard to picture my foster parents at Dun Alyn. And harder still to remember that they left here more than fifteen years ago to live in exile so that I would be safe. If Ogern had known that I existed, Miquain and I would both have been in danger. Our bard has sung the story twice since I arrived, but it still seems unreal—as if it had happened to someone else.

"I'll leave you to finish," Spusscio says, heading for the door. "Then let's meet with your father and consider the problem of Sorcha."

For the second part of the lesson, I demonstrate the changing trick. With Rory as my opponent, I feint to draw his sword far to his right, then whirl out of range, drop my shield, and move back with my sword in the other hand. Even though he realizes what I'm doing, I'm able to reach behind his shield and touch his right side with my blade.

"Practice that," I say. "You must learn to move very quickly at just the right moment. You'll all try it tomorrow."

Spusscio appears as they are leaving, and the two of us,

with Machonna between us, go directly to my father's chamber, where we find him gazing into the fire. This is not the first time I've seen him sitting motionless, deep in some reverie that he does not share with anyone.

When we're seated on the wide bedplace and he has turned his chair to face us, Spusscio describes Sorcha's behavior.

Belert confirms her claim. "Sorcha's grandfather had planned for her to spend part of this winter at Dun Struan. I saw no reason to object when she asked me for an escort; I hope her absence will give Ilena time to win over the other young people." He reaches down to pet Machonna, who has settled at his feet.

"It may help her to get away for a time," I say, remembering the sympathy I felt when I saw her grief over her grandfather's death. "When will she return?"

"By Imbolc," Belert says.

Imbolc is the time the ewes give birth and women celebrate the rites that keep us safe in childbirth; by then the worst of winter is over, though snow and cold often linger for another month or more. "Is travel possible at that time?" I ask, thinking of Durant.

"Dun Struan is only one day away, and there are no mountains to cross," Belert replies. "The cold water at the Ford of Dee is the only problem, but the river is low before the spring thaw."

"I've told you, Belert," Spusscio says, "that nothing good will come of contact with Dun Struan."

"I realize that, but I see no reason to prevent normal interactions between our fortresses." My father stares straight at Spusscio as if to challenge him to disagree.

Spusscio's face shows his anger, but his voice is courteous—almost too courteous—when he answers. "Of course, Belert. I'm sure your decision is wise."

✳ ✳ ✳

I keep Machonna in my room for the night. It is good to have company, and his furry body is warm against my feet. I am tired from the long day, but I find that sleep escapes me as I think of Durant and wonder where he camps tonight.

I think too of Sorcha. Her hatred of me is chilling. She has lost both her grandfather and a place as chief of Dun Alyn because of me. But I would not give up my position here for anything in the world.

Chapter 2

The long cold winter drags on. The last traveler to arrive from the West before the trail is completely closed is our new Druid, Gillis. He is young to be a Druid—no older, I'd guess, than Durant—but he has the air of authority common to his profession. Most in the fortress are pleased that he also follows the new religion.

He arrives well before midwinter eve and so is here to lead us to the oak grove where he cuts the sacred mistletoe. We put it above our doors and windows and in the barns and kennels to keep all of us and our animals safe through the winter.

It is far colder here than it was in the Vale of Enfert. I learn to wear two cloaks, and I often sleep in my fur-lined boots. We range farther and farther on our hunting parties since many animals have moved to warmer places for the winter. On days that we don't hunt, my students and I continue weapons instruction.

Sorcha returns from her trip to Dun Struan a few days after Imbolc, and I think the visit was good for her. She seems to have overcome her grief. She attends weapons practice every day and proves to be my best pupil. I often spar with her myself, as she is more than a match for the others.

She eats with us in the Great Hall and assumes a bright smile whenever she is around me. However, I have seen the anger in her eyes when she didn't know I was observing her, and I am still uneasy around her.

Gradually the days lengthen and soft sunshine breaks the gloom of winter. The snow cover on the mountains to the west melts farther and farther until at last the passes open so that travelers can get to us. A bard arrives with news of Saxon movements along the southern coast of Britain, and a monk visits and holds services for those of us who wish to attend.

But Durant does not come.

One afternoon I walk eastward on the wall, enjoying the clean spring breeze that freshens the smoky air. Dun Alyn sits high atop a promontory that juts out into the sea. After my childhood far to the west in a valley surrounded by mountains, I never tire of this view—water and sky to the eastern horizon and the rugged coastline of northern Britain stretching south and north as far as I can see.

Smoke filters through the thatched roofs of homes throughout the compound as people in from the fields stir their hearth fires to life against the evening chill; cooks' helpers turn spits of venison haunches and birds above the firepit outside the main kitchen. A young woman rakes loaves of bread out of an oven onto a plank and carries it into the Great Hall. I can hear herd dogs and the high voices of the children who are driving our cattle in from the meadow to the night pens.

It is pleasant up here a little above the commotion; if Durant were beside me, I would be content. Everyone in the fortress and in our territory outside the walls looks forward to our wedding feast. Some think that Arthur himself might come.

There is a mournful howl as Machonna finds me. I look down at the bristly white muzzle pointed in my direction and call, "All right, Machonna. I'm coming." As I head toward the ladder with the hound racing back and forth below me, I hear a shout from a sentry on the north wall.

"Riders!"

It must be Durant at last!

A sentry at the front gate takes up the call. "Riders. An armed troop!"

I turn and look down the trail to the south. There is no one in sight.

The trumpeter stationed over the front gate blows an alarm, and activity erupts in the courtyard below.

The first sentry calls again. "Riders from the north. They fly a blue pennant—with a brown wolf."

It can't be Durant. He would not come from the north, and I don't recognize that pennant. I pull his ring out from under my tunic and hold it tightly for reassurance. He will arrive soon; I know he will. Someone is coming up the ladder, so I put ring and chain out of sight and try to hide my disappointment.

Sorcha climbs up beside me. "Faolan! It's Faolan," she yells. Her face is brighter than I've ever seen it. She has spoken often of Faolan since she returned from Dun Struan, but I have not met him.

We stand together and watch the band approach; there are twelve in the group, and one of them leads a lovely little black colt. The two of us hurry down the ladder and join my father near the inner gate.

One of the visitors calls out, "Faolan—of Dun Struan!"

My father responds, "Dun Struan is welcome at Dun Alyn."

While our visitors are negotiating the entrances, everyone in the fortress who isn't bustling about preparing for guests gathers to see them.

Faolan is only a little taller than I am. Still, he is an impressive figure. His hair is loose about his shoulders and has the vivid stripes of an experienced warrior: glossy chestnut colored at the crown, deep auburn shading into reds and oranges through the midlength, and gold fading to light yellow at the tips. Long ago all the warriors of Britain molded their hair into a stiff ruff about their heads with a paste of lime and water when they prepared for battle. Now the custom is found only in a few tribes of the North. Those who practice it stand out because their hair has colorful stripes bleached in successive summers by the lime.

Despite the warm spring sun, he wears a wolfskin cloak. A wolf tail totem circles his left upper arm, and a gold chain and pendant hang over the cords that close his tunic. His bootlaces are tipped with the clawed feet of a small animal. Blue tattoos decorate his face and arms, and his chestnut mustache flows around his mouth and droops below his chin. His brown stallion is saddled over a bright blue cloth, and gold fittings decorate the leather harness straps.

He greets Belert first. "Blessings on this house and all who live in it. It has been too long since Dun Struan and Dun Alyn have feasted together."

"Blessings on the feet that brought you, Faolan," Belert responds. "It has been two years at least. How is your mother, the lady Edana?"

"She is well. Both she and my sister, Blath, send greetings to you and to the lady Ilena."

I'm not sure about this man. It is expected that a warrior will be confident, but Faolan's bold stare makes me uncomfortable. One glance at Sorcha tells me that she finds him pleasing.

He signals to one of his followers, and the young woman

22

steps forward, leading the black colt. Faolan takes the rein and, with a slight bow, hands it to Belert. "A gift," he says.

A horse is the traditional bride gift brought by a suitor to the father or guardian of the young woman he desires. Sorcha's face shines with pleasure, and Belert smiles at her as he takes the colt's rein.

Faolan steps back beside his saddle pack and reaches into it. "And for the lady herself . . ." He pulls out a gold bracelet and holds it up so that sunlight catches the twining decorations worked around it.

Machonna has pressed against my leg since I came off the wall. Now, as Faolan steps forward, the dog moves toward him and growls. I lean down to grasp his collar and look up again to find the gold bangle on Faolan's outstretched palm. I stare for a few moments at the strong warrior's hand and the dragon tattoo that snakes its way up the sun-browned arm. Machonna growls more loudly, and I jerk him back to sit beside me.

"Will you accept this, Lady Ilena?" Faolan asks. "And consider it a token of my request for our betrothal."

All fall silent around us. Even the horses stand quietly while I try to interpret this unexpected offer. I look to Belert and find no help. He stares straight forward with the aloof expression he often wears in public when he wants to conceal his feelings.

I catch a glimpse of Sorcha as she turns away into the crowd. There are tears on her cheeks, and her face is pale.

I reach out and touch the gold with my fingertip. "It is beautiful, Faolan. A gift far too fine for me." I do not pick it up.

Those behind me are shifting to let someone through; Machonna turns and whips his big tail in welcome as Spusscio pushes past to stand between me and our visitors.

He and Faolan face each other in silence for a time.

"What brings you to Dun Alyn?" Spusscio finally says. "Your usual trails lie farther north."

Faolan's eyes narrow, and he presses his lips together as if to keep from answering. When he does respond, his voice sounds forced. "In times like these it is wise to renew old friendships. And besides"—he makes a point of looking around Spusscio to see me—"I've heard much of the lady Ilena's beauty; those who spoke did not exaggerate."

I'm annoyed to feel myself flushing. I do not know this wolf-man, and I don't wish to show any reaction to his compliments. I think hard for an appropriate remark, but thankfully Belert takes over.

"Enough talk. We've kept our guests standing for too long." He turns to Cormec, who is our doorkeeper and thus responsible for matters of hospitality. "Are accommodations ready?"

"Of course," Cormec says. "Rooms are being prepared, and water is heating."

Belert speaks to Faolan. "I'll take you to the men's guest quarters, and Ilena will show the women to their rooms.

We'll wait for you in the Great Hall, where food will be ready by the time you've refreshed yourselves." Before Belert turns to lead the way across the compound, he stares at Spusscio, but I still can't tell what he is thinking. Faolan holds the bracelet out to me for another brief moment, then carries it away as he follows Belert.

Servants have opened chambers in the women's house, and we have our guests settled quickly. "Come to the Great Hall when you are ready," I say before hurrying back to my room.

As Machonna and I cross the central hearth area of our living quarters, I'm startled by loud voices in Belert's room. In the months I've lived here, I've never heard him yell at Spusscio, nor have I heard Spusscio's voice raised in anger at anyone.

"By the gods, Spusscio, you're not thinking clearly."

"There is no thinking about this. The man is as wily as the wolf he's named for."

"He came to the gate and asked admission. Of course I welcomed him. You know the laws of hospitality as well as I do."

"He wants Dun Alyn."

"I will not give him Dun Alyn! He made a formal betrothal request, and we must treat that with courtesy. I do not intend to insult a neighbor by refusing to meet with him."

Spusscio is near the door now. I hasten to my room, but

once inside I stay near the wicker wall between it and Belert's chamber. Spusscio's voice is clear as he takes his leave. "Neighbors, indeed! I've told you how he deals with neighbors. You trust that one at your peril."

I can hear his footsteps as he stomps out of the building. There is silence from Belert's side of the wall for a short time. Then, as I am considering whether to take my questions to him, he calls me.

"Ilena, will you come here, please?"

I sit down across from him, and Machonna settles at my feet.

"Faolan is a problem," he begins. "He courted your sister two years ago, but fortunately she too was betrothed to someone else. He and his father before him have tried to reunite our families, as did Ogern."

"At first I thought that Faolan had come for Sorcha," I say.

"So did I, but Sorcha does not have Dun Alyn as dowry, and you do."

"I am pledged to Durant," I say, "and I won't change my mind."

Belert smiles. "I didn't think you would."

"Can't we just tell him about Durant? Wouldn't Sorcha have told him already?"

"There are customs to be followed. Since Durant is not here, and you are not already married, the betrothal request is reasonable. We cannot take it lightly without insulting Faolan and all of Dun Struan."

I feel a jolt of fear and bend to pet Machonna to hide my face while I calm myself. More than one young woman has had to marry someone she didn't love in order to fulfill political strategies of the families involved. I wish Durant would arrive.

When I raise my head, Belert looks sympathetic. He reaches out and puts his hand over mine as he says, "I do not intend for you to marry Faolan. But we must turn him down in such a way that he has no complaint about it. If there is trouble between us, it will be because of Faolan's action and not because we have violated our old traditions."

"I could hear Spusscio," I admit. "He doesn't seem to care about traditions."

"Spusscio is not the chief of this fortress. His advice is invaluable, but he has his own reasons to hate Faolan. We will attempt to settle this peacefully. We'll meet with Faolan at half till noon tomorrow. Now let us go to dinner and show proper hospitality to our guests."

The Great Hall is full when I enter. Our bard is settled just below the head table and strums a peaceful melody on his harp. Faolan sits on Belert's right, and Sorcha is beside Faolan. There is no sign of the anger she showed when he handed me the bracelet; the two of them whisper together like old friends.

I speak to the other guests from Dun Struan as I pass the table where they're seated. "Are your quarters comfortable? Do you lack anything?"

When they've assured me that all is well and that they are honored to be our guests, I turn to the head table. Faolan is staring at me with the same bold gaze I found so disturbing at the gate. He smiles and raises his tankard to drink, still watching me over its rim. As the highest-ranking woman in the hall, it is my responsibility to honor an important guest by serving him, so I reach for his tankard.

"You are the most beautiful ale bringer that I have seen." His hand brushes mine, on purpose, I'm sure, as he hands it to me.

I keep a smile on my face. "Welcome to this hall. Dun Alyn is honored by your presence."

Gillis is the last to arrive at the head table. When he is seated, Belert signals the servers, and the meal begins. Spusscio does not appear at his place beside me, and I do not see him anywhere in the hall.

When Faolan's tankard is empty again, Sorcha leaps up to refill it, and once, when I have failed to notice that Belert's is empty, she refills his also. She tosses her head and smiles at me, clearly enjoying the opportunity to take over my duties.

I remember Belert's words about hospitality and try to concentrate on being a proper hostess, but I still picture that gold bracelet gleaming in the afternoon sun.

The evening ends at last. When Faolan, swaying from the ale he has consumed, moves toward me, I smile politely and hurry around the end of the table. When I look back from the door, he and Sorcha are walking away from the table together. Gillis has moved to a seat next to Belert, and the two of them are deep in conversation.

I go into Belert's room and try to calm myself while I wait for him.

When he arrives, he doesn't look surprised to see me. "I'm glad you're here, Ilena. We should talk about the meeting with Faolan tomorrow."

"His attention distresses me. I am uncomfortable around him," I say, "and why does Spusscio hate him so much?"

"Tell her, Belert!"

I didn't hear Spusscio come in, and I jump in surprise when he speaks.

He still wears his cloak, and he brings the scent of cold outside air into the room. "Or shall I?"

"It is your story, old friend. Not mine."

He hangs his cloak on a peg beside the door before taking a seat on a bench across the table from me. The fire makes a comfortable crackling noise, and the darkness around us makes our small firelit space seem a friendly refuge.

"My family had holdings north of River Dee, near Dun Struan's territory. My brother, Marrec, was younger than I." He looks down at the table and we wait. When he continues, his voice is sadder than I've ever heard it. "He was handsome and the joy of my parents' lives; I'm sure they had feared that he too might be a dwarf, but we all rejoiced when we saw that he was growing normally. He was betrothed to Faolan's sister, the dower heiress of Dun Struan, when both of them were young.

"My parents sent me to Gorre to study with Dubric, the head Druid of Britain. Though I could not be a Druid, my father was sure that knowledge would help me compensate for my size. Since there was no female heir in our family and my brother would be a chief of Dun Struan, I would rule our small fortress.

"I came home early the spring that they were married and celebrated with all of our people and with those of Dun Struan. Faolan was young, but already a warrior; he seemed courteous enough, and his parents, like mine, were happy with the union. I returned to Gorre in the fall and had no news of things at home all winter." He stops talking and turns to stare into the fire.

"This is painful for you," Belert says. "Go on to bed; I can tell Ilena the rest."

"I need to remember it," Spusscio says. He turns back to face us and continues. "When I came into our territory in early summer, I stopped to greet one of our farm families. They told me what had happened." He stops, and we wait in silence till he begins again. "Faolan's father had died of an illness in the winter. According to our customs, Marrec, as

30

husband of the dower heiress, became a chief at that time; he would assist his mother-in-law in ruling Dun Struan.

"In the spring Andrina, Faolan's cousin from Dun Lachan, had come for a visit. One day the three of them, Marrec, Faolan, and Andrina, rode out to hunt. When they returned, Marrec was dead—of a fall from his horse, they said.

"And soon after, a band of warriors attacked my home; my parents were killed along with everyone in the fortress, the livestock driven off, and the buildings put to the torch. The farmer told me that Faolan came to him a few days later and ordered him to muster and pay tribute at Dun Struan from then on.

"I went to the place where our fortress had stood and saw the ruins exactly as the farmer had described. With no home, no war band, and no hope of avenging my family, I wandered all summer, sheltering with friends for a night or camping in the forest."

"And then, thank the gods, you came here," Belert says.

"Aye," Spusscio says. "And found a home."

I've heard stories of raids on fortresses and of families wiped out, but I cannot think of anything to say to Spusscio. I reach across the table and cover his hand with mine. No wonder he hates Faolan.

I remember the way Faolan looked at me and shiver. I'll be glad when he is gone.

Chapter 3

When I enter Belert's chamber for our midmorning meeting, my father stands at the window with his hands behind his back; sunlight glances off his head, highlighting the gray in his hair.

Gillis arrives next. It is necessary for our Druid to be present when something as important as a betrothal is discussed. He alone knows all the laws, and he will be witness to whatever is said. "Greetings and God's blessing to you both," he says.

"And to you," I reply.

Belert turns away from the window and joins us at the table.

We hear footsteps, and I stand to greet Faolan.

He does not wear the wolfskin cloak today, and he has exchanged the gold pendant for an elaborately enameled piece. He nods to Belert and Gillis and takes a seat beside me on the bench.

Gillis begins, as is proper in important meetings, with a recitation of our family members. As I listen to the names and the relationships, I remember Moren telling me stories of these people—preparing me, though I didn't realize it at the time, for my role as chief of Dun Alyn. Gillis works his way back to Faolan's and my great-great grandparents, Sionnha and Ruarc, before he stops to summarize.

"The two of you are members of an ancient family that existed here before the Romans came. Your mothers and grandmothers and their mothers and grandmothers for nine generations and more have been chiefs of these lands. Your fathers, grandfathers, and the fathers of your grandfathers for nine generations have been heroes, brave fighters, and champions in the halls where they have feasted.

"A union between you would bring together two branches of an honorable old family and would make a formidable alliance here on the eastern seacoast." He pauses and looks at me.

I keep my face still so that no emotion shows. I understand now how important it is for such delicate matters as a betrothal request or, especially, a betrothal refusal to be handled with dignity and attention to the honor of the families involved.

"The laws are clear that such a suit deserves serious consideration and is not to be denied lightly," Gillis says. "But the laws are also clear that a prior betrothal cannot be set aside without proper reason and recompense to the other party."

He looks at me sternly. "Lady Ilena, do you wish to break your promise of marriage to Durant of Hadel in order to make union with Faolan of Dun Struan?"

I hesitate to be sure my voice is calm and courteous. I avoid Faolan's gaze and keep my eyes on Gillis as I answer. "I am betrothed to Durant of Hadel, and I do not wish to break that vow."

Gillis nods and turns to Belert. "Our customs require that a maiden's father be consulted. If you wish Ilena to break her vows with Durant, then you must speak now, and I will talk with the two of you to see whose wishes will prevail."

Belert does not waver. "Ilena is betrothed to Durant of Hadel. I have given my consent and my blessing to the union. Between God and myself, I will honor that agreement."

Faolan has been sitting still without speaking, but now he rises and says, "Durant of Hadel is from the South. For generations his family has allied with our enemies. His great-great grandfather was a member of the Roman legions! Such men do not belong here in the North."

Belert nods. "What you say has merit, but things have changed in Britain. We face new enemies from across the water. The old alliances are important, but so are new alliances that present a strong united front against the invaders."

"The Saxons have come by invitation of the old chiefs. There is room for them." Faolan's voice rises as he continues. "The families that have descended from Sionnha and her husband, Ruarc, belong together. A marriage between us is proper."

"A marriage between you and Ilena would indeed be proper," Gillis says, "but the lady Ilena is betrothed. That is a sacred vow and not to be set aside without good reason."

Faolan braces his arms on the table and leans closer to Belert; he stares from him to me and then to Gillis as he speaks. "I will not withdraw my offer. Who knows whether Durant will come back or not? He rides far and meets many people going about Arthur's business. He may have more important things to do than risking travel in the North for a woman he knew for only a short time."

I study his face, searching for the meaning behind his words. Is Durant in danger from Faolan? Or could he be right? Could Durant have changed his mind? I take a deep breath and try to draw strength from the weight of the ring against my chest.

Gillis watches me closely as he responds. "I have not met Durant, but the men who ride with Arthur are men of honor. I am sure that he would have sent word if he did not intend to keep his commitment to Ilena."

"Hah!" Faolan barks as he shoves his end of the bench

back and stomps to the door. He turns and adds more quietly, "If indeed Durant appears, send word to Dun Struan, and I will come to the wedding feast—in peace—to drink to your marriage. If he does not appear by the time the Beltaine fires are laid, you will hear from me again."

After he leaves, the three of us look at one another without speaking. I'm shaken by the malice in Faolan's voice when he spoke of Durant and annoyed by his arrogance in pursuing a betrothal that neither Belert nor I desire.

Gillis breaks the silence. "Arthur expects a move against his alliance in the North early this spring, perhaps right after Beltaine."

Belert says, "This is probably the beginning, then."

I cannot sit still any longer. "If you don't need me, Father?" I say.

He shakes his head, and I turn to Gillis. "If you will excuse me . . . ?"

He nods. "Try not to worry, Ilena. And stay out of Faolan's way while he's here."

"Gladly!" I say.

I head for the stables. A ride on the meadow with the wind and the sound of the ocean against the cliffs will calm me and clear my head. Rol whickers as I enter, and I head for his stall.

The black colt is in the stall next to his. "Hello," I say, and stretch my hand over the wall. The colt eyes me warily and backs away.

"I won't hurt you, pretty fellow," I say. I open the stall gate and move inside, but keep away from him. I want him to take a step toward me. He stretches his head and sniffs; I think he is ready to move in my direction, but then he looks at something behind me and shrinks back against the stall wall.

"His name is Dubh." Faolan came in so quietly that I didn't hear him. He opens the gate and joins me in the stall. "He has the best of our bloodlines; his dam is from the warm lands on the Mediterranean, and his sire's sire came from Gaul."

"He is a beauty," I say, stepping as far from Faolan as I can. Dubh stays against the wall, watching Faolan, while Rol peers through the wicker between the stalls.

"Come here," Faolan says, and grasps the colt's halter. Dubh rolls his eyes and tries to pull away. "Let the lady pet you." Faolan jerks the halter, and the colt stands trembling beside me.

"There, there," I say. "It's all right. I won't hurt you." I can feel him quivering as I stroke him. "I'll let you go. Don't tremble so."

Faolan laughs. "Horses need firmness, not petting. He'll come around with some training."

"Perhaps," I say, turning to leave the stall. "Our stable-master is gentle with them, and they seem to thrive."

The stall gate is ajar, but Faolan has stepped in front of the opening and blocks my exit. "You've affection enough for a colt, but you show none to me." There's an edge to his voice that worries me.

I try to sound pleasant when I reply. "I've told you; I'm betrothed. I keep my affection for one man alone."

He continues to block my path. "A woman like you needs a man of the North. Arthur's men are hardly men at all—soft, most of them, without the vigor to wed a lass like you."

I toss my head and raise my voice. "Let me pass, Faolan. I've no wish to wed you."

He laughs and moves as if to let me out of the stall, but when I brush against him to pass through the narrow opening in the gate, he seizes me and pulls me to him.

"Don't!" I cry out as I push him away.

He starts toward me again.

I draw my dirk and shift into a fighting stance.

He acknowledges the weapon with a nod and reaches for the dagger on his own belt. "As you wish, Lady Ilena."

His mocking tone tells me that he has no fear of my blade. I realize with a sinking feeling that, despite my hours of dirk practice with Moren, I may be no match for this experienced fighter.

I move toward him, and he turns his body away from my weapon, raising his left arm to deflect a strike. His back is to the open gate. As we shift positions, I glimpse a familiar figure—Machonna.

The dog is racing down the aisle so fast that I would

not have time to call out a warning if I wanted to. When he reaches the stall gate, he springs and lands on Faolan's shoulders, driving the man facedown into the straw on the floor.

I leap sideways just in time to avoid being knocked down by the two of them. Faolan's dirk flies from his hand and clatters against the wall beside the terrified colt.

Machonna is growling and barking fiercely now, trying to grasp his prey by the neck. "Off, Machonna!" I order. "Back!"

The colt whinnies in high shrieks, and Rol rears and trumpets on his side of the stall partition. Other horses stamp and whinny, answering Rol with their own fighting calls. The kennels just outside the stable door erupt into loud barks and howls.

I struggle to keep Machonna's teeth away from Faolan's neck, though I don't attempt to drag the dog completely off him.

Spusscio's voice rises above the noise. "Ilena! Where are you?" He rushes into the stall with his sword in hand. The stablemaster is close behind him.

I sheathe my dirk, then pull the hound completely off his victim and drag him out into the passageway.

Faolan, freed from the weight on his back, leaps for his dirk and wheels around with it at the ready. He looks surprised to find Spusscio in front of him with his sword raised to strike. The two stand unmoving for a few moments. The stablemaster is breathing hard as he keeps his staff up, ready to support Spusscio.

Rol can see me now and has stopped trumpeting. The other horses and the hounds are quieting. I keep a firm hand on Machonna's collar and try to gain control of myself. I don't know whether I'm trembling more from my anger at Faolan's insolence or from my unexpected fear when I saw how eager he was to fight.

Faolan looks from Spusscio to the stablemaster and then to me. He manages a grimace that might be a smile. "The lady does not take a compliment with good manners." He slips his dirk into its case and nods to Spusscio, who lowers his sword and steps out of the way. As Faolan passes me in the aisle, Machonna growls and tries to jerk free of my grasp. "That's a vicious animal," he says. "You should get rid of him."

I won't stoop to exchanging insults with the man and force myself to keep silent while he makes his way out of the barn.

Spusscio and I leave the stablemaster calming Dubh and take Machonna to the kennels. "I'm glad the hound was running free," I say, "and that you came when you did."

"How did you end up alone with him?" he asks.

"I stopped to pet the colt," I say. "Then I drew my dirk to defend myself."

Spusscio stops and turns to face me. "You drew your dirk

against Faolan? That's foolhardy! The man is known for the number of warriors he's killed in close combat."

I gulp. "I wondered why he seemed so pleased."

We find Belert in his quarters. When he's heard the story from each of us, he scowls at me. "You've no business being alone. It's not safe."

"This is my home," I say. "Surely I don't need an escort in my own stables."

"It sounds like you did today," he says. His voice softens, but he is firm. "From now on, Ilena, be careful when we have visitors, and do not go outside the fortress anymore without an armed companion."

"You must think of the future of Dun Alyn," Spusscio adds.

I want to protest, but I know what they mean. There are many stories of fortresses that have been conquered by force. If Faolan's advances had been successful, he would have a strong claim over me and Dun Alyn.

When I hear the sound of a horse troop gathering near the gate, I stay inside so that I won't have to see Faolan again.

At dinner Spusscio tells me that Sorcha has gone with them.

Chapter 4

We had been busy with the chores of early spring before Faolan came. Tools must be repaired and sharpened. Fields must be plowed and spread with manure from the barns and paddocks. Weapons, chariots, and harnesses are readied in spring because the season of battles comes soon after planting.

But now, since Faolan's attack on me, his threat to return at Beltaine, and his abrupt departure, we work with a new sense of urgency to ready ourselves for whatever troubles may come.

Still, I find time every afternoon to walk the ramparts, looking to the south with the hope that I'll see Durant riding his gray stallion out of the tree cover and onto the trail that leads to our gate. Each day I become more distressed that he has not come. Often I find myself staring at the horses on the red ring stone as if the smooth figures hold the answers to my questions.

Faolan's words haunt me. Perhaps Durant has changed his mind. Surely in that case, he would have sent a message.

It is more likely that something has happened to him. The fear grows day by day until I cannot escape it. I awaken frightened in the night, and a sense of dread keeps me company through the days. I cannot forget Spusscio's story. Faolan seemed sure that Durant would not come, and he may well have stopped him.

Gillis joins me one afternoon as I sit on the low wall that rims the seaside rampart, trying to take comfort from the calm blues that stretch to the horizon. I've become so intent on the rhythm of the waves marching toward me and crashing against the rocks below that I don't hear his footsteps until he is almost beside me.

He sits down a short distance away and looks out on the sea also. There is the faint sound of metal striking metal from the blacksmith's building, and Machonna keeps up a low howl below us. Gillis says, "You have come up here every afternoon all spring."

"Aye," I say.

"The scouts returned this afternoon," he says. "Spusscio and I sent them out several days ago to search for any sign of Durant."

I'm surprised. "I didn't know that."

"We hoped to have good news for you."

I brace myself. It is clear from his expression that there is no good news.

"They ranged beyond Dun Dreug and south on the western trail; that would have been his route from Uxelodunum."

"He might have come through Cameliard if Arthur had business there."

He shakes his head. "He stayed with a farmer a day's ride from Dun Dreug."

"When?"

"It was the waning half moon. Probably fifteen nights ago."

"And so he should be here." The fear swells inside me until I think I can't contain it. I glance down at the waves below and wonder how it would feel to be washed away—if that would end the pain.

"He did not arrive at Dun Dreug. The scouts inquired north along the trail also, but no one had seen him."

"Where does that trail to the north lead?"

"Dun Lachan—Andrina, cousin to Faolan on his father's side, is chief there. It is her sister, Camilla, who married a Saxon and rules Alcluith to the south."

I remember Moren's distress when he heard about Alcluith: "One of our most important fortresses! How could a British family allow their daughter to marry a Saxon?" He grumbled for days. I realize now what a sacrifice it was for him to remain in hiding in the Vale of Enfert when danger threatened Britain.

But my concern is for Durant. "Would Arthur have sent Durant to Dun Lachan?"

"It's not likely. Dun Lachan was the first of the far northern fortresses to invite Saxons into an alliance, and it is still one of the strongest. Saxon warriors quarter there to assist Andrina's war bands, and Saxon families have settled on the outskirts of Dun Lachan's territory. It would be far too dangerous for anyone from Arthur's table to come into the area."

"Durant is used to danger; traveling to far places alone is his custom."

"Yes, that's true." Gillis does not sound convinced.

"Perhaps he has business somewhere we haven't thought of, and he will come here when it is finished." I do not believe this even as I say it.

Gillis's stern expression has softened a little, and I think I see sympathy. "Let's go down now; Machonna is impatient."

I try to smile, but it is a weak effort.

✻ ✻ ✻

Three days before Beltaine, wood and grasses are piled high in readiness for the fires that will burn to purify our land and our livestock, and I lead a hunting party to secure game for the feast. We return in late afternoon and are tending to our horses in the stables when a messenger arrives. He calls out the traditional request for entering a hostile fortress.

"I bring word from Dun Struan. May I enter with a promise of safety?"

I reach the gate before Belert and Spusscio, who are hurrying out of the family quarters, and give the proper response. "A messenger need fear no harm at Dun Alyn. I am Ilena, chief of this fortress, and I guarantee your safety inside these walls."

I remember this young man from Faolan's visit. He dismounts and looks around uneasily at the sentries and the gathering crowd as though fearful of attack. At last he faces me and announces, "I am Gerden of Faolan's house guard."

Belert has come up beside me. "You need not fear treachery at Dun Alyn. We will hear you speak after you have eaten and refreshed yourself, and you will leave tomorrow morning as you have come."

"Unlike the custom in some places," Spusscio mutters.

The Great Hall fills rapidly as everyone crowds in to hear the message. It is clear from the young man's request for a guarantee of safety that it will be a challenge.

When Gerden has eaten a trencher of stew, he rises from the bench where he was sitting and comes to stand before Belert and me. He has calmed himself, and he speaks now in a steady voice.

"Will the chiefs of Dun Alyn hear what Faolan has charged me to say?"

Belert nods.

"Faolan reminds you that you insulted him in years past when he requested Miquain in marriage."

There is a slight rustle in the hall as people shift on their seats and stretch to see around those in front of them. I console myself with the knowledge that my father is as opposed to my marriage to Faolan as he was to my sister's and try to relax.

Gerden continues. "He believes that Dun Struan and Dun Alyn are natural allies, bound by the generations of those who lived before us. It is right that the families be united in marriage."

He pauses, and I can see that he is struggling to remember the exact words he has memorized. Belert sits, unmoving, with a face like stone; I try to copy him, but my mind churns with anxiety. The horrible story of Spusscio's brother, the memory of Faolan's attack in the stable, and my fear that Durant will never come all tumble around in my head.

"Faolan will come six days following Beltaine to claim his wife." Gerden takes another deep breath, glancing quickly at me and then back to Belert. "The lady Ilena is to be ready. If the gates of Dun Alyn open to us, we will join in a wedding feast. If they do not, we will . . ." He gulps. "We will enter Dun Alyn by whatever means we must and take Faolan's rightful bride."

A chill runs through my body and gathers like a lump of ice in my belly.

Belert rises. His voice thunders across the Great Hall with each word separate and clear. "The lady Ilena does not desire marriage to Faolan. She is betrothed to Durant, chief of Hadel in the South and follower of Arthur. Tell Faolan that he comes against Dun Alyn at his peril."

Gerden nods and sighs. "I will carry that message." He steps back and waits to be dismissed.

"Go," Belert says. "Cormec will show you to your quarters." He looks out across the room. "Gerden of Dun Struan is our guest and has been promised safety in this fortress."

People along the aisle to the door shift their feet to clear a path as Gerden leaves. There are no threats or gestures, but the faces that turn to follow his progress are grim.

Dinner is a solemn affair. Everyone in the fortress knows what Gerden's message was and what inevitable events our answer has put into action.

✳ ✳ ✳

After dinner, Gillis returns to the family quarters with Belert, Spusscio, and me. We gather around the table in Belert's chamber.

Spusscio begins. "I've received word of a buildup of

Saxon forces at Dun Lachan. If Andrina brings her own war band, along with the Saxon warriors who've gathered there, to assist Faolan, we'll have a fight on our hands."

"And I'm sure that she will," Gillis says. "This isn't a dispute between two neighboring fortresses; it is part of the plan by Saxons, and the Britons who conspire with them, to defeat Arthur's alliance and take over all of Britain. There isn't time to get Arthur here unless you intend to wait inside Dun Alyn and let Dun Struan lay siege."

Belert shakes his head. "No. We'll not risk getting hemmed in. It would take days to get word to Arthur and as many more days for him to arrive—if he were free to come to us. If Faolan and Andrina want a fight, we'll take one to them at the Ford of Dee."

I nod. Battles are often fought at fords because rivers are the natural boundaries of our territories. The rivers themselves belong to no one, so they and their crossings are neutral ground.

"I've four scouts ready to leave at dawn for our friends' fortresses," Spusscio says. "Two will go to Dun Dreug and two will ride northwest to Glein and Dun Selig. What word shall I send? And do you want the beacons tonight?"

"Aye," Belert says. "One beacon at each station to let our people know that trouble is coming; then, on the night after Beltaine, we'll light two at each place for an immediate muster. Tell Dreug, Glein, and Selig that Faolan has challenged us, and that we'll be at the Ford of Dee on the fourth night after Beltaine. They'll know they are needed. We'll meet tomorrow to decide who goes with us and who stays here." He turns to me. "What about your students?"

"They're ready to take their places in the war band," I say. I hope that I've prepared them well enough.

And that I am prepared myself.

Chapter 5

The day we set out for the Ford of Dee is overcast with a cold rain that stops and begins again time after time. The grounds of Dun Alyn are so crowded with people who've come inside for safety that it is difficult to get our horses and equipment through the clutter of pens, carts, and makeshift shelters.

We leave a holding force. Our youngsters are skilled with slings, and many men and women who would find the trip to the Ford of Dee difficult are still vigorous enough to wield a spear or sword in defense of their home. Those who remain behind line the path from the entrance out to the trail to wish us all well and, in many cases, to grasp a loved one's hand one more time.

I am amazed at the size of our troops. Cormec and Spusscio ride ahead with the scouts, and Belert, Gillis, and I follow. We are flanked by guards, and one holds Dun Alyn's banner high over our heads. The white goshawk on a black background flutters and snaps in the brisk wind.

We have a horse troop of fifty behind us with at least two hundred spear carriers and slingers behind them. They are followed by supply wagons, donkeys laden with blacksmiths' wares and tools, and chariots to transport our wounded back to Dun Alyn.

I am proud to see my students throughout the horse troops—all except Sorcha, who has cast her lot with Faolan.

The terrain is rough with hills and small streams, but the trip goes smoothly. Rol prances happily, showing his pleasure at the outing by tossing his head and rolling his eyes at Belert's mare. We are in place a short distance south of the Dee well before twilight. We make our night fires at the edge of a woods; boys and girls who've come to tend the horses help us rub down and feed our animals while others hurry to gather buckets of water from a stream that rushes along on its journey to the Dee.

I have just settled on a rock to eat the dried venison and bread that I carried in my pack when I hear a shout. "Someone comes. A troop, from the west."

I lay down my food and stand to draw my sword.

The sentry is stationed high on a cliff overlooking the

area. Her voice is drowned out by the noise of people readying their weapons.

"Silence!" Belert shouts. "I can't hear her."

"A large troop. They fly a green pennant with brown on it. And another follows—a blue pennant."

Allies! I replace my sword. Dun Dreug's banner is a gold boar on a blue background, and Glein flies the brown bear on green.

Perr of Dun Dreug is the first chief to join us. His voice is as hearty as I recall. "Ho! Belert. Spusscio. And the lovely lady Ilena!" He settles his sturdy frame on a log seat and sighs. "I'm tired of a saddle already. Getting old, I fear."

Belert laughs. "Not yet, my friend. It is good to see you."

Perr turns to me with a serious expression. "Have you heard anything about Durant?"

I shake my head. "Nothing," I say.

Doldalf of Dun Selig and Lenora of Glein arrive together. I stand to greet them, and Lenora wraps me in an enthusiastic embrace. "I've thought of you all winter," she says, "but especially since we heard about Durant." She releases me and looks at Spusscio. "Still no news?"

"Nothing," he says.

Doldalf grumbles, "There's too much activity on the trails this spring to suit me. Northerners going south, Saxons going north. No one's safe anymore."

Last fall when we needed help at Dun Alyn, these three

friends along with Durant and Hoel rode to our assistance. It is good to see them again.

We are in a large clearing near the stream, and our cheerful fire brightens the shadows as the sun drops below cliffs to the west. It could be a happy gathering of friends met to hunt if I did not know what lay ahead. By this time tomorrow we will be checking our weapons for the last time, preparing ourselves for battle.

"When do you expect Faolan?" Perr asks.

"We think that they will leave their fortress the day after tomorrow," I say.

"It is a short ride from Dun Struan to the ford, so we should see them by midmorning," Spusscio says.

We are not disturbed during the night, and when I awaken, people are cleaning and polishing their weapons and seeing to belt and harness fittings. The horses are corralled in a makeshift paddock well away from the large clear area between woods and riverbank.

After breakfast Spusscio says, "I'm going up there to look over the area." He nods toward a large hill in the distance. "Who wants to join me?"

Gillis, Lenora, and I follow him, and by a little before noon, we are standing on an outcrop that gives a good view of the countryside.

"That's Dun Struan," Spusscio says. He points to the northeast where a cloud of smoke from cooking fires hovers above a fortress. We can see the walls and three huge earthen rings that surround them, but little else because we are so far away.

The river Dee runs below us, churning between steep rocky banks to the west, slowing as it approaches the ford, and widening out as it moves toward the sea. Lenora stares at it for a long time.

"Can it be forded anywhere downstream?" she asks.

"No," Spusscio says. "It is wide and the sands are treacherous. This is the lowest crossing, and there are no others for a great distance upstream because it flows swiftly between high banks for much of its length."

"Then we need not fear a surprise attack," she says.

"No," he answers. "There is no other route for them but across that ford."

When we return to the campsite, I see that Belert has ordered drivers to move the wagons and chariots back along the trail and to space themselves out so that our warriors will have room to move to the rear if they need to.

The mood around the campfires during dinner and throughout the evening is somber, though no one seems eager to sleep. At last, as the fires die down, and the moon rises above the treetops, I can stay awake no longer.

"A good night to you all," I say, and roll myself in my cloak with my feet toward the fire and my head pillowed on my war vest. I can hear the others around me following my example, and finally talking ceases throughout the camp area. I sleep fitfully, partly because of the hard ground beneath me—I've become too accustomed to my soft bed—but also because thoughts of tomorrow's battle stir me awake each time I drop into slumber.

Will I be equal to the role of chief? I know what a warrior must do, and I know how to fight as well as any here. But will I be strong enough in the face of a large force against us? Can I hold my position at Belert's right hand?

As a chief myself, I am charged with duties of leadership and example far beyond the other warriors. Since this is my first battle with the war band of Dun Alyn, my every move will be scrutinized, and the judgment passed on my qualifications will follow me for years.

At last my thoughts fade so I can sleep, and I awaken as dawn is casting a pink glow against the clouds. I look toward the two watchmen stationed on the cliff and see them staring across the river. Belert and Spusscio stand on a small rise nearby, looking in the same direction. When I reach them, I see two horsemen on the north bank of Dee. They watch us for a time, then turn their horses back toward Dun Struan.

"Scouts," Spusscio says.

"Aye," Belert says, "their main troop will be along soon." He pulls his sword from its scabbard and raises the blade above his head. He turns slowly in a complete circle and moves back into the ranks of warriors, brandishing the sword in a silent and unmistakable signal to prepare for battle. The other chiefs, weapons high, move among their troops with the same message.

I hurry back to my sleeping place to gather up my cloak and pack, then carry them into the woods out of the way. Those who wear the traditional long wool garment strip it off and toss it onto piles of others. Most wear leather trousers, but some do not have even that much clothing when the woolen cloak is gone. Lenora wears a tunic over her trousers, as do I, and both of us have thick leather vests for protection.

Fear is building inside me, and I wish for a moment that I were back safely in the Vale of Enfert, where my only opponents were the wild boars and the sheaves of straw Moren hung for targets.

A shout rings out from the cliff above us. Gillis stands with his arms raised and his head back. He begins an ancient plea to the gods of our ancestors, then looks down and points at me. People have pressed forward into the clearing to hear him, and now they begin to chant my name.

"Lady Ilena, Lady Ilena." It begins quietly from a few people, then builds until the surrounding forest seems to echo it.

I know it is customary to honor a leader before going into battle, but Belert is here, and Doldalf and Perr and Lenora. I am the youngest chief, and this is my first battle. Surely I should not stand beside the Druid. Belert nods at me, and I can see that he is saying, "Go!"

Lenora smiles and reaches out to take my arm. "Come, Ilena. You are chief of Dun Alyn. Your people want to see their leader." She leads me through an aisle that opens in the crowd until we reach the trail to the cliff top. There she releases my arm and gives me a gentle push.

I climb the steep path with the sound of my name roaring around me. "Ilena. Ilena. Ilena, Chief Ilena!"

Gillis waits while I pull myself up the last steps onto the cliff top and then turns to the crowd again with his arms raised. I hold my sword up as Belert did earlier and listen to the voices. As I hear my name mixed with the battle cries of four different fortresses, I feel a surge of power. My fear is gone now, replaced by the assurance that I can do what I must. I step forward to the edge of the cliff and brandish my sword in a wide circle over my head.

When Gillis speaks into my ear, "It is enough. We must prepare our ranks," I lower my arm and look across the river.

Faolan rides toward the ford, with Sorcha on his right. A warrior on his left holds the brown and blue wolf head pennant so that it streams over them. There is a chariot with three people directly behind him, and ranks of warriors, the bright morning sun gleaming off their weapons, stretch back along the trail as far as I can see.

I raise my sword again, throw my head back, and call the battle cry of Dun Alyn with all my strength.

Chapter 6

Our war bands are forming along the edge of the clearing and back into the woods. The chiefs, our house guards, and the sword carriers will lead against the first attack. Horse tenders are hurrying our mounts to us. I take Rol's rein from the girl who leads him and swing into the saddle. We will fight on horseback for as long as we can.

"Try to get him when I dismount," I say.

"Yes, lady. I'll be nearby," she says. She reaches out and touches my hand briefly. "God's blessing on you."

I nod my thanks, pull my helmet from its place on the harness and tug it on, then move Rol forward to a position between Belert and Perr.

Spusscio, still on foot, rushes toward us, his boots and trousers dripping wet. "Andrina! Andrina is here."

"The witch!" Perr says.

"Aye," Belert says, "and no surprise. Gillis warned us."

"Are there other fortresses?" I ask.

"Probably," Spusscio answers. "Dun Lachan has plenty of allies, and I'm sure there are Saxons along too."

I'm glad that our own friends have come to help us.

Faolan moves forward to the riverbank, and we all quiet to hear him. "My cousins of Dun Alyn! Again I bring the gifts." He turns and a young girl leads the black colt forward. "Consider my request. There should be only friendship between our people." He wears neither tunic nor vest, and his hair stands out in a lime-stiffened ruff around his head. The blue tattoos on his bare upper body ripple as he lifts the gold bracelet.

Rol moves sideways as Gillis rides up between Perr and me. The Druid's face is stern, and his long hair blows loose around his head.

"Ilena," Faolan continues. "Accept your bride gifts and your destiny. Save your people and mine from the bloody wounds of war."

I swallow hard. I do not wish to marry Faolan, but I do not want my people harmed on my account.

Belert senses my hesitation and reaches out to hold Rol's rein. "Do not waver, Daughter. You know of his treachery.

60

He would force Dun Alyn to bow to Saxons, and Dreug, and the others would fall without us."

Gillis urges his horse forward. He moves down onto the riverbank on our side and raises his voice until all in both front ranks can hear him. "I am Gillis, Druid of Dun Alyn. I warn you that the gods favor Arthur and his followers. If you attack us, you abandon the gods who have cared for Britons for ages past, and you anger the true God who is above them all."

A team of black horses pulls a chariot forward, and the woman in it steps up beside her driver, leaving a man standing alone behind them. She wears a war helmet, but her black hair streams out around it; her arm, brandishing her sword over her head, is muscular and browned from the sun. She speaks loudly above the noise of the river and the stamp of horses and the clank of battle gear. "Gillis, I know well that you have forsaken the old ways. The gods of our ancestors lead us to make peace with the Saxons and to resist the southern traitor, Arthur."

Belert leans closer to me and says, "Andrina!"

Faolan points to the trees that line the river. "The Morrigan have gathered." Ravens have settled onto branches throughout the area, and more are arriving in waves overhead. "They wait for the feast that simmers for them."

"It is you, Faolan, who have called them," Belert shouts.

Gillis returns to us and takes his place beside me; I am on Belert's right and Spusscio is on his left. Our best warriors push forward to circle us. Perr is swept off into the center of his own troops.

I breathe a prayer for our protection and for my own courage as the front line of Dun Struan's forces plunges into the river to meet our front line with a great clash of swords and spears. Battle cries from both sides rise above the din.

I snatch my sword into my left hand to wipe my palm against my leather vest, then grasp the hilt again with my right hand. Faolan, with Andrina's chariot beside him, has crossed the river and is pushing through our ring of warriors toward us.

"Now, Faolan," I mutter, "we face each other again." My fear has retreated and a cold rage at the man who brings this threat against us has taken its place. I urge Rol forward to intercept him.

Faolan swerves out of my path, and Andrina's chariot rushes toward me. As she approaches, the driver turns so that I am heading straight for the warrior who stands beside her.

The sounds of battle blur as I recognize Durant.

Rol stops abruptly and rears upward. I can hear myself screaming Durant's name again and again as the chariot thunders past us and disappears into the midst of Dun Struan's warriors.

I sit motionless, staring after them, while the fight swirls around me. When I come to my senses, the front line of battle has moved into the river, and I am far behind with the foot troops pressing around me.

"Belert!" Where is he? "Belert!" Shock and shame overcome me. I have abandoned my chief.

A warrior can commit no greater sin.

I hold Rol still for a moment, hoping that somehow I can disappear—be spirited by some otherworldly force up and away from this place. I see Rory battling a Northern warrior; the two of them move back and forth over a slick patch of mud at the river's edge. Suddenly Rory slips and stumbles off balance. As he tries to recover his footing, I break free of my trance.

I raise my sword and urge Rol toward the river, reaching Rory just as he falls to one knee. My sword stroke severs his opponent's head, and Rol's charge carries me out into the river. We plunge into a group of Northmen who surround four warriors from Dun Dreug. I leave two of the Northmen sprawled in the water and the others scattering from my path.

Only my death can wipe out my guilt, and I court that death. Wherever the fighting is fiercest, I force Rol on with my sword whirling and my voice raised in the war cry of Dun Alyn.

At last I see Belert with Spusscio at his side. Faolan and four others surround them.

I drive into the group with such force that two of Dun Struan's warriors fall under Rol's hooves and Belert and Spusscio are pushed aside. When Faolan leaps down from his horse and swings his sword at Rol's forelegs, I whirl the horse out of danger and jump to the ground to engage Faolan.

He moves toward me with the mocking smile I remember from the stables at Dun Alyn. "Where is your wolf-dog now, Lady Ilena?" he asks.

In answer I leap forward with my sword swinging in a wide arc. He has his shield in place in time and attempts to strike me as I complete the move. Instead of checking my swing as he expects, I let my sword stroke pull me around in a complete circle and dodge out of his range. As he turns to follow me, I try to slash below his shield, but he defends himself well.

His back is to the river, and I'm able to press him bit by bit until he stands on slippery mud. "Will you yield now, Faolan?" I say. "Your forces are retreating across the river."

His eyes dart away from me for a moment, but he looks back immediately and says, "That's an old trick, Ilena." He lunges in my direction with his sword raised, but one foot slips, and he loses momentum.

As he steps back farther, searching for firmer footing, I'm pushed aside by Andrina's chariot. Only she and her driver are in the vehicle now. I try to slash her as she passes, but she is moving too fast.

The chariot slows, and she jumps down from the back, sword in hand. Out of the corner of my eye, I see Faolan and two of his warriors being pushed back by Lenora and a group from Glein. Andrina moves to join them, and I go after her.

"Turn and face me," I demand. "Where is Durant? What have you done with him?"

She laughs. "You should have accepted Faolan."

We face each other in knee-deep water. There are few of either side still on horseback now, and the clang of weapons and the cries of the wounded rise together above the sound of the river and the croaks of the waiting ravens.

Andrina stands firmly on a flat part of the river bottom, her dark eyes staring into mine. I step slowly around her, trying to lure her into swinging her sword. She is good; she has the patience to wait till I make a move and then slash when I am off balance. I wait also. It seems an eternity that we circle and stare and attempt brief false moves to lure the other into an attack.

I dare not take my eyes off her face to see how the battle is going, but the area around us seems to be opening up, with fewer and fewer people pressing around us. I move forward one step and force Andrina back; none of her warriors are behind her for support. I do not know if any from Dun Alyn are near me. As I attempt to push her another step toward the north bank of the river, she lunges forward, aiming for my left side.

I twist quickly so that her sword glances off my shield without harming me; at the same time I strike toward her shield. As soon as she turns to protect herself, I check my movement and thrust in behind the shield from the other side. My sword fails to penetrate her heavy leather vest and glances downward, slashing her trousers and drawing blood.

She gasps and steps backward again. Three warriors from Dun Struan rush to her aid and begin pushing me back. Spusscio appears on my right side and Cormec on my left. Steadily we move the Dun Struan band toward the north bank. Andrina falters as the injured leg buckles. One of her companions catches her and helps her away. The other two turn and retreat.

"Come back!" Spusscio says. He takes my arm and tries to lead me to the south bank of Dee. "Stay with your troops. Faolan is withdrawing."

I pause to look around. The dead and wounded of both sides lie on the banks and in the river; the water rushing downstream around my boots is bright red. Dun Struan's forces are in full retreat.

"No!" I yell. I jerk free of Spusscio's grasp and charge through the bloody water in pursuit of Andrina and Faolan. I hope to fight my way through their ranks and find Durant.

Belert rides in front of me and halts his horse in my path. "It's enough, Ilena. Let them go." He waits until Spusscio and Cormec catch up with me and says to them, "Get her back to camp and stay with her till she calms down. I'm looking for Perr." He watches me with a solemn expression on his face, then adds, "I'll talk with you later."

I try to hold his gaze to learn what he is thinking, but I drop my eyes in shame after a few moments. Thank God he is unhurt, but I can take no credit for that.

When Spusscio and Cormec take my arms, I let them lead me back through the river to our campfire.

"Sit here!" Spusscio says. "Pull off your boots and warm your feet. I'll get you ale."

I want to argue, but I've begun trembling so hard that I can't talk. I drop onto a flat rock and try to remove my boots, but my hands won't serve me. Cormec stoops to pull them off. I nod my thanks and try to control my shaking jaw and chattering teeth.

The ale is strong, not yet mixed with water. I choke and sputter but manage to swallow two large gulps.

Spusscio takes the aleskin from me and says, "I'll get it back to the surgeons." He looks at Cormec. "Stay with her."

I rub my arms and begin to feel calmer. Two of our warriors go by with another who's bleeding freely from a wound in his arm. All three of them glance in my direction but hurry on without acknowledging me. Cormec is silent. When I look up again, Spusscio has returned. I suspect that the two of them are staying close to protect me.

Perr and Lenora walk by without stopping. Perr jerks his head away when he sees me; Lenora hesitates but then walks on with him.

I cannot bear to stay out here where everyone can see me.

I stand and wait for a moment to be sure I'm steady on my feet. "I'm going back into the woods," I say. "I want my cloak. You are both needed here. I'll be all right."

When I reach the cover of the trees, I look back and see that they are watching me. Spusscio has such a bleak expression that I can hardly stand it.

It is long past noon now, but the sun is still bright in the western sky. Here under the trees, shafts of sunlight bring some relief from the gloom of deep woods. I find my cloak and pack where I left them and give thanks that no one else is around. I realize that I am still gripping my sword tightly in my right hand, and I look at the gory blade. It should be washed in the river, but I do not want to walk back through our people again. I break fresh leaves off a low-hanging branch of an ancient oak and clean the blade as much as possible before putting it into the scabbard. I stand the weapon against a stump, then lower myself to the ground and lean back against a tree.

I don't know how long I sit without moving, trying not to think about the battle, about that moment when I fell back away from my chief. I force myself to try to blot out the image of Durant at Andrina's side.

His ring is heavy against my chest, and I pull it out to look at the red horses. One looks straight toward me, but stare as I may into the half-closed eyes, I can learn nothing from the stone.

Wagon and chariot wheels creak along the trail as the wounded are carried to the surgery at the rear. At least one wagon will be gathering our dead to take them back to Dun Alyn for the funeral fire.

I should be walking among the warriors, asking about each one, visiting the wounded, and thanking those who came from other fortresses to our aid—if I were worthy to be chief. But I cannot show my face now. I've given up all right to lead, and if the old laws prevail, I will give up my life for my offense.

No one comes to speak with me for a long time. Finally I hear footfalls nearby and turn to see Belert approaching. He carries a waterskin and a loaf of bread.

"Have you eaten?" he asks. His voice is kind.

I shake my head. "I have bread, but no appetite."

"You must eat something. We will leave at first light in the morning." He is silent for a few minutes, then sighs and sits down beside me. He breaks off a piece of the bread and hands it to me.

"It is not unusual to freeze with fright in your first battle."

"But I am . . . was . . . a chief," I say.

"I should not have kept you beside me. The first wave of an attack is frightening, and only experienced warriors can hold firm. I forgot that you had not seen a full battle before."

"But I was not frightened," I say. "Oh, perhaps at first, before they started toward us, but that faded at once. I was calm and ready for anything—I thought. I never expected to see him here, and the shock stunned me for a time."

Belert looks puzzled. "Him?"

"Durant."

He stares at me in silence for several moments, then speaks carefully, slowly, as one speaks to a child. "Where did you see Durant?"

"Behind Andrina. He was the third person in the chariot; I didn't recognize him until the driver swerved so that Durant was directly in front of me."

"Are you sure?"

"Of course," I say.

"Sometimes things seem to appear when we want them too much," he says.

"I certainly didn't want Durant riding beside an enemy chief," I snap. "Faolan rode toward us, and I pushed ahead of you to shield you. I know my duty. I am—was—proud to ride on your sword side."

"Did you feel fear then?"

"No!" The question angers me. "I have faced enemies before. I welcomed the thought of combat with Faolan. He has earned my hatred."

"As Faolan approached, someone else broke through the line around us and I went to Spusscio's aid, leaving Faolan to you. Did you engage him?"

"No. He swerved just out of sword range and turned back into his ranks. Andrina's chariot was behind him, and it kept coming. As it reached me, it too swerved and turned across my path. Durant was an arm's length away."

"Why do you think it was Durant?"

"I know it was." I think about the man I saw. "I wouldn't mistake Durant even with the helmet covering so much of his face. It could not have been anyone else."

He sighs heavily. "I do not know what this means. The law . . ."

"I know what the law says."

He pulls himself up and looks beyond me. "I cannot bear to lose you, too."

I bow my head and bite my lip to keep from crying. I've not only disgraced myself, but I've brought more sorrow to my father.

He reaches out and pulls me up beside him. "I must go. Perr and the others are waiting."

I lean against him with my face mashed into his leather war vest for a moment, then gulp and pull myself away. "I'm sorry, Father. I wish that I could relive those moments."

"Be strong, Ilena." He tries to smile, then turns and leaves me.

No one else comes until nearly dark. I've gathered wood for a night fire and am dragging last summer's oak leaves into a pile for a bed when Gillis arrives. I think for a moment that he must have waited till dark, when no one would see him talking with me, but a closer look at his tired face and bloodstained clothing tells me that I've misjudged him.

"I would have come sooner," he begins, "but the surgery is busy."

"I should have come," I say. But should I have? Would I have been welcome? Finally I confess, "I didn't know what to do."

He lowers himself to the ground by the fire and leans his chin on his drawn-up knees. "I almost sent for you, but I feared that some would resent your presence. The story of the first moments of battle has spread throughout our camps."

"I'm sure that it has."

"Word of your courage and your fighting frenzy when you recovered yourself has also spread. People are not sure what to think."

I sigh. "Nor am I. I thought I could trust myself in the face of danger. But to see him—"

He interrupts me. "Belert told me your story."

"It was Durant." I say it firmly, but even as I speak, doubts creep in. It was someone or something with Durant's appearance, but I did not touch him or hear his voice or see his eyes.

"Andrina is a witch; she has more knowledge of herbs, spirits, and the ways of the otherworld than anyone I know. She was at the Druid school for a time when I was there. She was a brilliant student, but she seemed to listen to voices that we did not hear. She is capable of tricking us, perhaps even of conspiring with someone of the otherworld."

"Do you believe that I saw Durant?"

He hesitates. "Andrina is skilled in magic arts and

could bewitch or drug a man, but there is a more likely explanation."

I wait while he shifts his body and stretches his legs toward the fire.

When he speaks, he watches me closely. "You are young, and you have suffered greatly. Surely Moren's death last fall, your journey to Dun Alyn and the dangers you met there, and Durant's absence are all weighing on you. It is not strange that you might see one you love while the rest of us do not."

"You think I imagined him!"

He does not look at me, but peers into the fire as if searching for meaning there. "Would he have allied with Andrina?"

I think hard. How well do I know Durant? Could he be a traitor to Arthur and to me? "I cannot believe that he would betray me. And it is impossible that he would betray Arthur."

Gillis stands, and though he faces me, I cannot see his expression clearly in the gloom. He speaks sternly. "The elders will meet to discuss your fate, and the warriors of Dun Alyn will be consulted. But the final judgment is mine."

I take a deep breath and try to keep my voice steady. "I know that death is the penalty for failing to defend a chief."

"Yes," he says, "but your father has asked mercy for you. I will review the laws carefully and seek signs to guide me.

Come into the Great Hall of Dun Alyn tomorrow at dinner-time prepared to hear my decision."

He turns and disappears into the forest. I wait, standing alone in the gathering darkness, until I can no longer hear his footsteps, then crumple onto my bed. I fall asleep quickly but waken again and again during the long night to stare at the full moon floating above the trees and think about my fate.

Chapter 7

Spusscio brings Rol to me in the early morning light. I can hear movement and the clink of harness fittings all around me, but no one else has come near me since Gillis left last night.

"Do you wish to join Belert?" he asks.

I hesitate. The joy of riding with my father at the head of our troops seems even sweeter now that it will be taken from me. Would it hurt to ride there just once more? Shame and concern for Belert's reputation give me the answer. "I'll come along at the rear," I say.

He nods and seems to look for words. Finally he says only, "As you wish."

At first I ride behind the foot troops, among the chariots

and wagons. Some of the wounded sit upright and watch our progress; others, too badly wounded to sit, lie drugged against the pain on the straw that covers the wagon and chariot beds. I fall farther and farther back until I am riding behind the last wagon, which holds three corpses laid side by side. Only the warriors of the rear guard are behind me.

I grieve for those we've lost, yet I envy them. How much better to go home to a hero's funeral than to ride disgraced toward a coward's death.

It is late afternoon when we reach Dun Alyn's gates. I enter last and lead Rol to his stall myself since the horse tenders are all busy. I take my time grooming him and bringing feed and water. Perhaps this is the last time I'll be with him. I throw my arms around his neck and lean against him, then leave the barn without looking back.

There is warm water in my room, and I wash carefully and comb my hair till it is smooth. I put on my blue dress and the girdle that my mother made for me. Before I toss the dirty bathwater out the window, I take my sword out of its scabbard and clean it thoroughly. After I've polished it with the linen bath towel, I stand it in its place in the corner.

I wonder if I will ever use it again.

Our bard is strumming a peaceful song as I approach the door of the hall, and I can hear conversation inside. Cormec is in his place as doorkeeper. He bows as he holds the doorskin aside for me.

There is total silence as I walk the aisle between the

tables. I do not look to the right or to the left, but keep my eyes on Belert at the head table. He is standing now, and Gillis stands beside him. Spusscio remains seated with his head bowed. The bard has stopped playing and holds his harp upright with his hands muffling the strings.

This story will be told in halls throughout Britain, and few who hear it will have any sympathy for me. I step onto the dais and stand before my father.

He sighs and turns to Gillis. "Have you made a decision?"

Gillis nods, and Belert sits down.

Gillis looks out over the room. "You have heard the story of the battle yesterday. Ilena faltered and fell to the rear when the attack came. She left her chief unprotected." He waits while voices murmur through the room. When it quiets, he resumes. "You watched her when the Northmen attacked Dun Alyn last fall, and you know of her courage. She has taught Dun Alyn's young people weaponry, and she has led the hunting bands against the wild boar and other game. You know, as do I, that she is brave, skilled in warfare, and loyal to her father, Chief Belert."

I stand still, watching him and listening for the sounds behind me. I can hear shuffling as someone stands to speak, and silence as people stop their conversations to listen.

"I have hunted with Chief Ilena." It is Cormec. "She shows more courage when she faces the wild boar than anyone I've followed. I do not know why she faltered at the Ford of Dee, but I would like to hear her story."

Gillis looks at me for a few moments, then responds. "Her story is a strange one. Ilena saw an apparition riding beside Andrina, an image of Durant; whether in the flesh or as a spirit, she could not determine. Since no one else saw him, it is possible that Andrina cast a spell on Ilena, or perhaps that Andrina has progressed far enough into the dark arts to conjure up one from the Sidhe to ride beside her."

The room erupts with excitement. Feet shuffle and benches creak as people stand to talk to others about the news.

Gillis stands, calm and powerful. Spusscio watches the movement in the hall. Belert toys with his dirk and stares beyond it at the tabletop. He looks weary, and he lays the dirk down for a moment to rub his eyes, then glances at me and manages a tiny smile. His eyes are warm as they have always been when he looks at me, and I feel reassured that he, at least, does not blame me for my actions.

Gillis clears his throat and raps his dirk on the table. People scurry to their benches, and quiet returns to the hall. "I have thought long about Ilena's situation," he begins.

"The penalty for falling behind in battle for any reason but grave injury is death." He pauses. "Ilena is guilty!

"The penalty when an uninjured warrior leaves a chief unprotected is death." He looks at me and then out into the hall. "Ilena is guilty!

"The penalty when a chief fails to lead the war band is death." This time when he pauses, the hall is so quiet I can hear the sound of the sea through the open window.

"Ilena is guilty!"

His words bash against me like physical blows. It is all that I can do to stand still and keep my head high. The room behind me remains silent.

Gillis continues. "Because of the strange circumstances of Ilena's lapse, because of her youth, and because her father, Chief Belert, asks mercy, I have spent the hours since the battle ended looking for another way.

"There are a few times—very few—in our history when the death penalty has not been exacted. The first requirement for setting it aside is that the Druid must certify that mercy is indicated.

"I believe that it is in this case and will so notify the Council of Druids.

"The second requirement is that you, Ilena's people, desire mercy."

A bench scrapes behind me as someone stands. "I stumbled during the battle yesterday." It is Rory. "Ilena saved my life. I will follow her gladly. She is a good chief and she deserves mercy."

Cormec's voice rings out. "I've spoken once of her courage; I will speak again. She fought like one of the old heroes at the Ford of Dee. It took three of us to stop her from following our opponents back into their own territory."

"Aye," someone calls. "I've not seen such a fine battle rage in my life."

There is a hum of conversation through the room.

Belert looks out at the crowd and then gives me a slight nod of encouragement. I feel some of the fear start to drain from my body.

Spusscio stands and waits for quiet before beginning. "Faolan and Andrina planned this. If Ilena is no longer chief of Dun Alyn, then Sorcha is the next heir, and Sorcha rides with Faolan now."

Someone in the back begins chanting, "Mercy! Mercy! Mercy for Chief Ilena!"

Others take up the call until the hall rings with it.

Gillis waits patiently for the chants to die down before he speaks again. "You have made a wise decision. Ilena is not a coward and does not deserve a coward's death. But the law must be satisfied."

He continues. "Ilena, you have heard your people."

"I have heard them," I say, "and I am grateful to them."

"You understand that I must pronounce a judgment to satisfy the law?"

"I do."

"The old codes provide two punishments other than death. You must choose between them. Turn now and face your people."

I do not want to look out over the hall, but I turn slowly and stand with my head held high and my fists clenched tightly at my sides.

Moren told me always to look brave and under control no matter how I felt. I breathe a prayer of thanks for him and for Grenna. They taught me well, and I only wish that I brought honor to their memory instead of disgrace.

Gillis's voice booms from behind me. "Ilena may stay at Dun Alyn and live out her life here—if she relinquishes her place as chief and does not ride with the war band again."

Give up being chief and riding with the war band? But that is my life. What would I do?

Rory is sitting at a front table, and I can see the shock on his face. There is a stir as others react.

Gillis raps on the table again. "That is one choice. The other"—he pauses until it is quiet—"is that Ilena must leave Dun Alyn—alone—and not return until she has accomplished tasks great enough to prove herself worthy to be chief of this fortress."

I'm stunned. Somehow I'd resigned myself to death, but the relief I felt when mercy was granted has turned to confusion.

A life of dishonor, being reminded every day that I failed as warrior and chief, while someone else—Sorcha?—rules? I prefer death!

Or exile, forced to go out alone in search of a hero's task. The prospect frightens me—but it is the only choice I can make.

"Have you decided?" Gillis asks.

The people in the hall seem to hold their breath, waiting for my reply.

"I am a warrior, and I am chief of Dun Alyn," I say. "I

81

have failed in my duty to you, but I will not give up that high honor for safety." I pause for a deep breath, then say firmly, "I choose exile!"

People throughout the hall murmur and shift in their seats. Rory at least approves. He is smiling and nodding.

"Wait, Ilena," Gillis says. "Consider carefully. This is a dangerous time in Britain. Your father and your friends will not know where you are or how you fare. If you choose exile, you might well be choosing death."

"I . . ." I start to say that I am sure, but I think of my father. He still grieves for my mother and sister. If my staying would bring him peace . . . I turn and face him. "Father." It is hard to get the words out, but I must. "Do you want me to stay?"

He looks at me sadly for a few moments, then says, "Of course I want you by my side, Ilena, as would any parent. But you are a warrior. The way of a warrior is a dangerous path and an honorable one. I would not ask you to forsake your life's calling. Go with my blessing."

I blink and try to smile my thanks. I look at Gillis and repeat, "I choose exile!"

"If you are sure," he says, "you must leave tomorrow. You may return when your deeds of valor can be told in this hall."

I hesitate for a moment, then bow to him and to my father before I turn back to my people. "I thank you all. I pray that your judgment is right and that I will deserve the mercy you have shown me."

I walk along the crowded aisle as proudly and as slowly as I can manage. At the door I stop to talk with Cormec. "Thank you for speaking," I say.

He nods solemnly. "What I said is true. You are a good chief and a courageous warrior. Come back safely to us."

"I hope to."

When I step outside, Machonna races toward me and leaps up to lick my face. My joy at seeing the dog fades as I think of leaving him tomorrow. He races happy circles around me all the way to my room.

I keep him with me for the night, and he sprawls at my feet as I burrow into the bedskins. My last thoughts before falling asleep are of this room and this luxurious bed. I do not know when I will sleep in warmth and comfort again.

I awaken before sunup and take Machonna out into the compound, then tie him securely so that he cannot follow me. I hug him hard and whisper, "Good-bye, friend."

When I return to my room, Belert is there, surveying the pack I've laid open on the bedplace, and the small pile of belongings that I've stacked in it.

"Do you have what you need?" he asks.

"I plan to take only what I brought with me from the Vale of Enfert," I say.

"Nonsense!" he says. "Everything here is yours." He

throws open the three larchwood boxes that stand along one side of the room and pulls a tangle of gold bangle bracelets and rings out of the smallest one. "You'll need these to buy food and shelter." He drops them onto the bedplace beside my pack and turns back to the larger box.

"And this!" He tosses the green dress onto the bedplace. "Chiefs and daughters of chiefs wear green." He takes my shoulders and pulls me around to face him.

"You are the daughter of Cara, chief of Dun Alyn, and her consort, Belert; your foster parents were Moren, noted war leader of Dun Alyn, and his wife, Grenna. That is as noble a lineage as any in Britain, and it is yours wherever you go, whatever you do. Do not forget it."

I've been thinking of myself as the girl I was in the Vale of Enfert with no knowledge of my lineage or of my proper place in life. I gulp and say, "Yes, Father. I'll remember."

"Now hurry. You are wise to get an early start." He picks up my sword from the corner and carries it out with him.

I tie straps around the pack and pick up my cloak and war helmet. I stand in the doorway, looking back at the room for several moments. I'd never seen such a fine chamber before I came to Dun Alyn. Will I live in this one again?

The courtyard is empty, though I can hear voices from the kitchen. I would like to gather some loaves and meat, but I don't want to face anyone. I go into the warm stable with its heavy scent of horses and hay.

"No! I forbid it!" Gillis is shouting at someone.

"She can't go alone!" Spusscio's voice is just as loud.

By the time I get to Rol's stall, the two of them have stopped yelling and are arguing in hushed tones. Belert is tightening Rol's saddle straps, and a good roan mare with a large pack is tied to the outside of the stall beside Rol's.

"The law is clear," Gillis says. "She will not redeem herself any other way."

"She'll be in danger every moment she's gone," Spusscio responds. "When Faolan and Andrina get wind of her exile—and they will somehow—they'll be after her at once."

Gillis sighs. "I know. But she must earn the respect of her people and of our allies. You heard Perr and Doldalf."

"I'll be fine," I say.

"I could go with you and no one would even know it. I come and go constantly on Belert's business." As he speaks, Spusscio takes my pack and secures it behind Rol's saddle.

How welcome his company would be!

"Gillis is right," Belert says. He puts his hand on my shoulder. "I would keep Ilena safe at Dun Alyn or go with her myself if it were possible. But she has chosen exile, and all we can do is wish her well."

"Thank you, Spusscio," I say. "I would like nothing better than your company, but I must go alone. I will return to you." I pray that this is true.

"Well, then," he says, "your horses are ready." He picks up three small loaves of bread and some meat strips from a clean pile of hay nearby and tucks them into the top of the pack on Rol's back. My sword and shield are in their places in the harness, and spears bristle from a case on Rol's side.

"There are more loaves and plenty of dried meat in the roan's pack," he adds. "And oats for the horses and some sleeping skins are there. And two containers of ale."

"Thank you," I say, touched by his work. I had expected to slip away without seeing anyone.

When we lead the horses out of the barn, the morning sun has cleared the walltop, and the entrance is open for the day. Gillis has gone ahead and waits for us at the gate.

I can hear Machonna howling from the kennels. I'd like to hug him good-bye one more time, but it would only make him more unhappy to have me leave him again. When I step back to mount Rol, Spusscio is watching.

I don't trust myself to speak, so I nod and swing onto Rol's back. Belert fastens the packhorse's lead rein onto my saddle, then stands with his hand on Rol's withers.

"I must go," I say.

"Yes." Belert blinks and pats Rol's neck. "Go with God and do not forget the path back to us." He reaches his hand up to me, and I grasp it and hold it against my face for a moment.

When I let go of his hand, I reach down to clasp Spusscio's. Then I straighten up and turn Rol toward the gate. I nod a greeting to the sentries and stop Rol beside Gillis.

"Thank you," I say. "I know that you have done what the law requires, but you have also given me hope."

He sighs. "I pray that you will be strong enough for whatever awaits you."

I do not look back until I am clear of all the entrances and well down the path onto level ground. That's when I hear a familiar sound behind me. Machonna, howling madly, is racing toward me. He wears his wide hunting collar with a new leash wrapped securely around it.

Spusscio is standing in the open inner gate of the fortress; Belert is up on the ramparts with Gillis beside him. I wave to them, then dismount to unwrap the leash and stow it in my pack.

I go on with Rol and the packhorse trotting smartly and Machonna running alongside.

There are no trails leading south of Dun Alyn because impassable marshes stretch from the shoreline to the mountains; the ocean is on our east, and Dun Struan and River Dee lie directly to the north. My only option is west over the mountains. There, past Dun Dreug and not far from the Vale of Enfert, lies the north-south trail.

Dun Lachan, Andrina's fortress, is somewhere along that path into the far North.

By the time I've crossed the first mountain range, my mind is made up. There may be no brave deeds there, but I must know why Durant was with Andrina. I will go to Dun Lachan.

The lengthening days of spring are a good time to travel, as dawn comes early and the long twilights will allow me to continue well into the night hours. I am almost halfway up the western range of mountains when I stop for the night.

Machonna stays close to me; he is used to forests and fortresses, and the stark emptiness of the mountain land-scape makes him nervous. After I water and feed the horses, I share bread and meat with him. Our tiny fire sends shadows over the cliffs, and the wind howls around the peaks. Despite my brave words this morning in the barn, I've never made night camp alone before, and I am glad that Machonna is with me. I sleep well and don't awaken until dawn.

It is not hard to get an early start when the only prepara-tion is to eat a little bread and harness the horses. We make good time over the mountain range and pass below Dun Dreug in midafternoon; I look up with longing at the fortress on the hilltop and wish that I could find a welcome there with hot food, a soft bed, and the companionship of friends. But I remember the way Chief Perr walked past me without speaking at the Ford of Dee and put the thought out of my mind.

I push us on as long as it is light enough to see the trail, so we make camp well west of Dun Dreug. We should reach the north-south trail early tomorrow morning. By nightfall it has begun to rain, and I find shelter in a clearing with a rock overhang that protects Machonna and me. I tie the horses nearby under thick evergreens that provide some cover for them.

Machonna is happy to be in a forest and dashes around our little clearing several times before I call him.

"Come, Machonna! Come here." He obeys reluctantly and puts his nose on his paws to watch me start a fire under the overhang and tend to the horses.

When I awaken sometime in the night, he is gone. I whistle for a time, then settle back onto my bed of damp pine branches. Hunting dogs are trained to range widely and return to their master; surely he will find his way back.

I am awakened again just as darkness begins to weaken in early morning. The horses are pulling against their reins, bending the saplings that I secured them to and bumping into each other in their alarm. The din sounds like the kennels at Dun Alyn when the dogs fight over their food, but there are no kennels here in the forest.

"Machonna!" I can't tell if any of the yelps and growls are his. "Machonna! Come!" I scoop up the casting spears that I keep beside me at night and race toward the noise.

As I stumble over tree roots and through underbrush, the yelps turn into howls of pain. I burst into a clearing in time to see three wolves vanishing into a thicket. Machonna, blood streaking his fur, tries to follow them, falls, then raises himself and tries again.

"Machonna! Wait!" He turns and stumbles toward me for a few steps, then collapses in a trembling heap. When I reach him, I can see that the blood comes from a wound on his left shoulder. The leather collar protected his throat, but there is a slash from the shoulder joint to his knee. His brown eyes fix on my face as if he's pleading with me to stop his pain.

"All right, boy," I say. "It'll be fine. Let's get you back to camp." I drop the spears and hoist him up. The jostling increases his pain, and he whimpers, but he does not resist as I get his front feet over my shoulder and lock my arms under his back haunches.

The big pack that Spusscio prepared contains what I need. I wash out Machonna's wound with a big splash from one of the aleskins and split a linen towel into strips for a bandage.

When I've cut as much hair away from the wound as I can and washed it out again, I pick woundwort, which is growing near the trail, and pack it into the gash, then wrap the bandage firmly around his leg. He has stopped struggling to get up, but he wheezes and whimpers while I work and falls asleep as soon as I finish.

I had hoped to be on my way north toward Dun Lachan soon after sunrise, but Machonna's wound is too serious for him to travel far. I fear that it won't heal for days. There are no houses in this area that I know of; it is too far to go back to Dun Alyn, and I doubt that I would be admitted at Dun Dreug.

There is only one place we can go—one place where I know I will be welcome. The Vale of Enfert lies less than a day from here. My childhood friends Fiona and Jon will care for Machonna. Their mother, Aten, is the village healer and knows the best herbs to heal a wound.

I repack the roan's bundles until there is a hollow space across the middle of the pack. Then I wrestle Machonna up into the depression and secure him with ropes so that he won't slip as we move.

"It's all right, boy," I say. "We're going home."

Chapter 8

It is almost evening when I stop at the head of the pass and look down over the valley where I grew up.

Memories flood my mind, and tears blur my vision. I stood like this so many times, resting from the climb up the steep path, often leading Rol with a deer or boar from the day's hunt slung over his saddle. I look down the trail into the village, almost expecting to see my foster mother, Grenna, hurrying out to greet me. But of course she died three years ago.

My old friend Fiona has seen me. Her voice floats up to me as she hurries along the path. "Ilena! Is it you?"

"Fiona!" I wave to her and start down the slope. My homeplace is high on the hillside to the left, closer to the pass than the rest of the village, but a large outcrop of rock hides it from my view. Jon, Fiona's brother, is probably busy in the paddock, opening the gate to the night pen or leading Legg, Moren's horse, into his stall in the barn. When I left last fall, I asked Jon to move in and care for the livestock and the fields until I returned—if I returned.

I urge Rol forward, eager to see Jon, but bracing myself for the possibility of finding a woman there also. When I refused Jon's proposal, I knew that one day he would marry someone else. A farmer needs a wife beside him, and Jon was eager to have a family of his own.

As I move past the boulders, I strain to see my old home in the deepening twilight. It takes a few moments for me to realize that it isn't there.

The comfortable house with its thatched roof is gone, as are the barn and other outbuildings. The paddock fence, woven from supple willow branches and repaired carefully each spring, has vanished. I stare in silence at the black patches and scorched posts that are all that is left of our farm.

Fiona has reached me and holds out her arm to help me dismount. "It's horrible!" she says.

"What happened?" I step into her embrace and close my eyes for a few moments to blot out the sight of devastation.

Aten joins us. "Welcome, Ilena," she says. "Though it's a sad homecoming we have for you." She looks tired, and she's thinner than she was last fall.

The three of us stand, arm in arm, looking at the burned-out homestead. "I don't understand," I say. "How could all the buildings have caught fire at once? The barn was well away from the house."

"They lit them all," Fiona says. "It was before Beltaine—fifteen days or so ago. Craig and I were down at the end of the village, working in our fields. We'd been married for just a short time." She stops and starts to sob.

Aten embraces her daughter for a moment, then takes up the story. "Jon and Kenna were living here; they were married soon after you left." She hesitates and watches to see how I react to the news.

I'm not surprised. Kenna made no secret of her feelings for Jon, and I'm sure the two of them are happy together. "Were either of them hurt? The buildings are a loss, but Jon can build new ones. Who lit them afire? And why?"

"Jon is gone." Fiona forces herself to stop crying and continues. "So is Craig. All of our men and the big boys, too."

"What happened?" I ask. Rol shakes his harness and nudges my back with his head. "Let's go down," I say. "The others are waiting." A group of women has gathered near Aten's house. Kenna, her belly swollen in pregnancy, is among them.

As we walk, Aten describes the group of warriors, most of them from somewhere in the North, Jon had said, and a few who spoke a language no one recognized. "They went into every house and field and forced all the men and boys to go with them."

"Except Eogan, who was hunting," Fiona says.

We reach the group at Aten's yard, and old friends surround me. Their greetings worry Machonna, who struggles against the ropes that hold him. Fiona helps me get him down, and I carry him into the house.

By the time Aten has examined Machonna's wound and applied a fresh dressing, Fiona and Kenna have Rol and the packhorse settled into Aten's small barn. It is getting dark as Aten dips soup for us. After we've eaten, the four of us sit on the bedplaces and talk long into the night.

"Tell me again," I say. "What happened first? Did the watch give alarm? How many were there?"

"I was here with Kenna," Aten begins. "There wasn't a watch yet since it was too early for the usual slave raiders, but Kenna and I heard the noise. They took the cow and calf and the pigs out of your barn—then fired the place. It was a great awful burning."

"Cryner?" I ask. An old dog is of little matter when human lives are endangered, but I hope the hound did not suffer.

"Gone," Kenna says. "In the winter. Just didn't wake up one morning. Jon carried him up the slope and buried him there near your folks."

"And Legg?" I asked. "Did they take him?"

"Eogan had him," Kenna says. "Hunting, like always."

I remember Eogan, a tall boy about two years younger than I. He spent a lot of time watching Moren teach me sword fighting, and he liked nothing better than permission to groom the horses. "He rides him, then?" I ask.

"Aye," Aten says. "Eogan has been our best hunter all winter. Thank the gods he at least is left to us."

"But Legg is no good at the plow or the mill," Kenna adds. "Tried him at both, Eogan did, but the horse wouldn't pull."

I picture the proud stallion harnessed like a donkey or an ox to the plow and shake my head. "It's not something he's trained for," I say. "So they took the oxen, too?"

"Aye," Aten says. "We've nothing to pull the plow or turn the millstones now but ourselves."

"What did the men do?" I ask. "Did they try to fight back?"

Aten shook her head. "Jon considered it, but the leader spoke to us." She stops, overcome with sadness, and adds, "There were about forty in the group."

"They'd kill us all and burn our homes like they had yours unless our men went with them," Fiona says.

"Eogan saw the fire and hurried back to us," Aten says, "but they were gone by the time he got here."

"We stopped him from going after them," Fiona says. "It wouldn't have helped, and we'd have lost him and the horse besides."

"It's hard for Eogan to do all the men's work alone, and

we're behind in plowing and planting," Aten says. "It's a bad time." She smiles at me. "But it is good to have you here."

We sit in silence, watching the hearth fire burn lower and lower. Machonna whimpers in his sleep, and a cow lows quietly from the barn. I've missed these small houses with the animals close by and the peaceful nighttime talk of crops and hunting. But the vale is no refuge now.

Kenna and Aten go outside to check the paddock gate for the night, and Fiona and I sit for a few more minutes by the remains of the fire.

I say, "I'll help where I can tomorrow."

"Will you stay, then?" Fiona asks. She sounds hopeful, and I'm reluctant to disappoint her, but I must.

"I cannot, Fiona. I'd planned to go directly on; I've business in the North."

"Perhaps you'll find word of our men." She sounds disappointed but resigned; she was the only person in the village who seemed to understand why I left last fall.

The four of us settle onto the bedplaces without any further conversation. I try to stay awake to think about Durant and about the problems here, but I can't keep my eyes open and soon fall into a sound sleep.

I waken to Machonna's whine. Aten has dressed his wound again, and he struggles to get up. "Can you lift him, Ilena?" she asks. "He needs to get outside for a bit, but he can't put weight on this yet."

97

I carry him out and stand him carefully in a sunny place. I yawn and stretch my muscles while he hobbles around sniffing grass and trying to relieve himself without leaning on his injured foreleg. The sun has cleared the mountains to the east, so I've slept long past daybreak.

Fiona comes from the barn as I'm lugging the dog inside. "Kenna is grooming Rol," she says, "and will rub the roan down too. How's the hound?"

"Good," I say. "It was hard to treat the wound on the trail, and the ride on horseback must have been painful for him, but he's better for a good night's sleep and your mother's care."

While Machonna laps at a bowl of water Fiona holds for him, I open my smaller pack and remove the remaining loaves of bread and strips of meat. I hand them to Aten. "There is more food in the big pack," I say, "and oats enough for the horses. We won't be a burden to you."

She smiles. "Grenna's child is not a burden to me."

Grenna's foster child, I think, but I do not say anything. That is a long story better kept for another time.

There's a noise at the door, and Eogan enters. He is taller than last fall, and he greets me with the direct gaze of an adult. "Well met, Ilena. It is good to see you again."

"And you, Eogan," I say. I hear a horse whicker and a harness jingle. "Is that Legg?" I hurry outside.

The stallion knows me and ducks his head to rub it against my shoulder. "He's sleek and well cared for," I say.

"Aye," Eogan says. "Jon let me groom and feed him every

98

day. And I've ridden him most days—so he'd stay strong, of course."

"Of course," I say. "It is good you've been able to keep him exercised. He looks ready for anything."

Eogan nods. His welcoming smile has faded. "He's fit as ever. And you'll have come for him, I suppose."

His affection for the horse is touching. "Do you think you could keep him longer? I've business in the North and don't need him at present."

He brightens at once. "Keep him longer? Yes! Our barn is a bit small, but I've made a separate stall where the roof is the highest and he can turn around and raise his head. He doesn't seem to mind the cow and the pigs."

I laugh. "I think he's happy with you. He looks content to me."

"Will you be at the gathering this afternoon?"

I hadn't heard of a gathering, but it is the custom whenever travelers arrive in the village for everyone to come to one home to meet them. "I'm sure that I will be," I say.

"I'm off to hunt," Eogan says. "We need meat with so much of the livestock gone."

"How much did you lose?" I ask.

"Everything from Jon's . . . your place, and whatever was still in night pens when they came. Youngsters had about half the cattle and most of the pigs out and up on the meadow." He gestures to the east of the village, where grassland stretches to hills at the end of the valley.

"And the oxen," I say. "I heard about them. Let's try the roan if we can rig a harness. She's trained for chariot work and might pull a plow."

"I'll get what I put together for Legg," he says. "The oxen yoke is of no use, of course." He turns to leave, then stops and faces me again. "I almost forgot. There was nothing left of your house and barn when the burning stopped, but I have Moren's scabbard and shield. They were with Legg's harness." He hesitates and looks down. "I would have returned them, but I wanted to study them for a time."

"I'm pleased that you have them," I say. "And have you room for them also?"

He nods vigorously and smiles. "Thank you, Ilena."

I spend the rest of the day leading, tugging, and coaxing the roan mare through the muck of a field. The wet black earth is cold on my bare feet, and the worn tunic that Aten found for me to wear is little protection against the cool spring breeze. I envy Eogan as he rides off on Legg with a bundle of hunting spears fastened to the horse's harness. I've done fieldwork before, of course, but by the time I was old enough to do hard work, my main job was hunting. The roan, however, seems afraid of the others, and only I can get her to lean into the makeshift harness around her chest and pull at the heavy plow behind her.

When I judge that the horse has worked as hard as she should for a day and call a halt, one field is finished and another started. I'm happy to join Fiona and the others in the icy stream to rinse away the dirt from our legs and arms.

"I've oats enough for her for a few days," I say, "but we'll need to find more grain if she's to work like this."

"Aye," Fiona says. "There's grain still in the pits. Show me how much she'll need each day, and I'll see to it. Can you leave her with us, then?"

I have little need for a pack animal if I carry only fighting gear, and it's better by far to be without one if I have to move fast. Besides, my old friends need her more than I do. "Yes, I can leave her. That should see you through the plowing at least."

"We've a bull yearling that Eogan thinks will pull at the millstone; the children can take turns pushing along with it so we can get some of the grinding done."

"Good," I say. "The mare can't handle that and plowing."

By the time I've fed and wiped down the roan, tended to Machonna, and changed back into my own clothes, there's a fire blazing at the storyteller's house, and a pot over it, sending the scent of stew wafting through the village. Aten, Fiona, Kenna, and I walk there together. I think of Durant and wonder where he eats his meal on this springtime evening. The others walk in silence too, grieving, I'm sure, for their missing husbands.

It is a gathering of women, with Eogan and the younger boys who surround him the only males present. Though I've talked with almost everyone at some time during the day, there is a stir of welcoming sounds when I arrive.

After we have eaten, Delya, the storyteller, begins. "We welcome Ilena home. Our grief for our husbands and sons and brothers is great, but with Ilena here our fears for our safety diminish."

There are nods and smiles throughout the group. I can see hope and—worse—trust in the faces of these women whom I've known all my life.

She continues. "When Moren and Grenna, with Ilena in her arms, joined us that chilly spring day so long ago, the dangers that had plagued us vanished; Moren's skill and courage kept the raiders away from then on. And now Ilena has returned just as we, defenseless, face the spring raiding season."

I want to scream, "No! I'm not staying. I have to find Durant." But I can't. I cannot watch the hope in their faces turn to anguish when they learn that I haven't come to help them. Fiona is looking in my direction, waiting for me to speak, but I sit silent and listen as the teller goes through the story of my family's life in the Vale of Enfert. When the group disbands, I hurry back to Aten's house as soon as I can.

I'm so tired from the fieldwork that I go to sleep quickly, but some time later I awaken. I try to go back to sleep, but I cannot relax on the hard straw bed. Images of Durant sweeping by me at the Ford of Dee come as they have most nights, but now I'm troubled by the plight of the folk here in Enfert, too. At last I get up and creep outside.

The half-moon, which lit our walk home from the gathering, has set, and the night sky is a sparkling sheet of stars. I locate the Great Bear and follow its direction to the North Star. I long to gather my things, harness Rol, and leave as soon as dawn shows the trail.

I find a fallen tree beside the meadow and sit to stare at the brilliant sky. When I was little, I would lie in the grass here with Jon and Fiona beside me, and we would tell each other stories about the pictures we could see in the heavens.

"Ilena?" Fiona's voice comes from somewhere in the darkness.

I stand and look around, but I can't see her. "Fiona? Over here."

"I missed you," she says. "I feared you might have left us already." She is beside me now.

"I'm sorry I woke you," I say. "I tried to slip out quietly."

"I haven't slept well since Craig and the others left," she says.

"I know. I lie awake too, thinking of a loved one."

"You've found someone?" Though it's too dark to see her face clearly, I sense that she is smiling.

"Aye," I say. We sit down close together on the log, and after a few minutes of silence, I begin to tell of my experiences since I left the vale last fall. She is entranced by the story of Durant. "And he is one of Arthur's friends?"

"A cousin. He rides at the Dragon Chief's sword side." Even in this isolated valley people hear tales brought by the bards, and so they know what an honor that is.

My description of the events at Dun Alyn amazes her. "You? Ilena—my friend—you are chief of a fortress?"

"I was," I say, and continue my tale.

When I've finished, she embraces me, and I feel her tears against my face.

"Of course your first allegiance is to your betrothed," she says. "I understand why you must go on."

"But I am worried about you here in Enfert, too."

"I'm not sure how we'll defend ourselves if the slave raiders from Eriu arrive," she says, "or if that band of Northerners and Saxons comes back."

I start to ask if they meet to practice with spears or slings, but I stop myself. I remember how difficult it was for Moren to interest the men in developing fighting skills, and the women in the vale have never considered using weapons.

She gets up. "I should sleep. I must work hard tomorrow. We are trying to do our own tasks and those of our husbands and fathers. Are you coming in now?"

"No," I say. "I'll be along in a few minutes."

As the stars wheel in their pattern through the springtime sky, I think about Durant and Dun Alyn and about this village. What I must do seems clear enough finally, though I do not like it.

Even though my position as chief of Dun Alyn is in doubt, it is my duty to fight for my people, to lead warriors, and to train others to handle weapons. The folk of Enfert are my people as certainly as are those of Dun Alyn. I failed at the Ford of Dee, but I must help my friends here.

I pull the gold chain from inside my tunic and hold Durant's ring while I think of our time together at Dun Alyn. Will I ever feel his arms around me again?

When dawn begins to light the eastern sky, I go back into the house and fall asleep at once. Aten and Fiona get up early, and I awaken to the smell of hot oatcakes on the stone at the inside hearth. Kenna is stirring herself on her bed across the room.

She sees that my eyes are open and smiles. "I am glad that you are here, Ilena. I've feared for my babe with no one to protect us. Now there is hope for us; perhaps we can survive until Jon and the others return."

Fiona is squatting beside the fire, turning the oatcakes. She stops her work and waits to hear how I will respond to Kenna.

I stand and stretch, then say, "I will stay here for a time; we must organize some defenses."

"With women and children?" Fiona asks.

I laugh. "Yes, Fiona. Except for Eogan, we are a village of women and children now. So we will do what we must."

Chapter 9

As I step into the yard, I see a familiar face peering over the gate. "Calum," I call. "Just who I need right now."

He grins and ducks his head as he comes in. "I'm on my way to gather the livestock—what we've got left, at least."

Calum is about nine and the liveliest of the village boys, a leader in any group of his companions whether they're tending the village herds or spying on couples who've sought a bit of privacy in the long summer evenings.

"Carry word for me to the mothers that I want every young person over four summers old on the meadow as soon as the sun is above that great oak." I point to a tall tree that stands at the eastern end of the valley. "Tell them the livestock can wait a bit this morning. And everyone should bring a sling if they can."

He nods vigorously and turns to leave. "One more thing," I say. "Find Eogan and tell him I need him."

The first group of youngsters arrives with Eogan in their midst. "You see that dead tree?" I ask the children. "I want you to practice hitting it with a slingstone." They jostle for position and begin. I step back to give them room and motion Eogan to join me.

"Will you be staying, then?" he asks.

"A while," I say. "You and I must form a defensive force for the village."

He looks startled, then squares his shoulders and smiles. "I've wondered what we could do." The children are milling about, either casting stones in the general direction of the dead tree or begging to borrow a sling from someone else. "It'll be hard to make a defensive force out of that," he says.

"Notice that they've made a great shield of stones even though few of them are near the target. No one could have walked safely across that space."

"Aye, that's right. A stone hurts no matter who casts it."

"Stop," I call. "No more slinging now. Go look for the stones. We can't afford to lose any. When you've gathered all that were cast, come sit here in front of me."

I send Eogan to bring the women, and I study the

children assembling before me. Fifteen have come, and I don't think any are missing.

When the last youngster has settled herself on the ground and placed her slingstones beside her in the grass, I say, "Calum is in charge of slingers. It is a big responsibility." Calum straightens up and looks solemn. "You are all to pay close attention to his directions. From now on no one is to leave the house without a sling and a pouch of slingstones. If you do not have them, talk to Macaulay."

Macaulay, whose father made most of the shoes and leather goods for the village, gives me a startled look, but listens as I continue. "Has your father taught you how to work leather?"

He nods slightly. "My mother knows more about it than I do."

"I'll talk to her. Between you, I hope you can furnish us with more slings and pouches.

"All of you must make sure that there is a pile of slingstones inside every door, every barn, and every compound gate. You should collect as many round stones as you can find, and, to be sure we have enough, Nessa will help us make more out of clay." Nessa is a tiny child, but I know that she has at least eight summers already. She keeps her round blue eyes on my face as I speak. "Nessa's father was . . . is our potter, as you all know. Nessa, did you help him find clay?"

"Yes, often. The best is outside the vale, along a stream to the west."

"Good," I say. "Calum will assign others to help you gather clay, and Eogan will go with you for protection. Then everyone will help make slingstones—perfectly round, remember—to be fired in the kiln."

"I'm not allowed near the kiln," Nessa says. "Though I've often watched from a distance."

"Your mother will help fire them, I'm sure." I look from one to another. "Does everyone understand what is to be done?" They all nod. "And how important it is that you get ready to defend our village?" They nod again. "Take the livestock out now, but don't forget to practice slinging and to look for stones."

When Eogan returns with the women, I explain what I've asked the children to do and remind them also to carry slings and pouches of stones wherever they go. "We must be ready to defend ourselves if we are attacked."

"Are slings enough?" Kenna asks. "I'm sure that we couldn't have stopped the war band that took Jon and the others with a few stones."

"No," I agree. "Probably not. But I don't think a band like that will come again. Most likely, their fortress needed extra workers during the battle season, and they found them here. They'll no doubt release everyone at summer's end because they won't want to feed extra people through the winter."

"I hope so," Fiona says.

"You must be able to fight off the raiding parties from

Eriu, who sail their leather boats into our waters and come ashore to plunder and to take slaves to sell in their country," I say. "That is a danger every year."

"And they do not return the children they steal!" Delya says.

"What about the watch?" Aten asks. "We haven't had one since the men left."

"I've tried," Eogan says. "I've slept up on the pass most nights, and I stayed during the day when I didn't need to hunt."

"Eogan will plan a schedule so that two people are always on sentry duty. He'll tell you your times," I say. "I know we must be in the fields soon, but I'd like you all here again after dinner for weapons practice—if you want to learn more about defending yourselves."

"I'll be here!" Aten says. "When I think of Jon and the others . . ."

"Aye," Kenna says. She puts her hand on her belly. "I will fight to keep my babe from harm."

"Then I will meet you here when we have eaten and cared for the animals. We'll work with staffs today, so bring a stout stick of some kind."

Fiona stays behind when the others leave. "It is good to plan what we can do. I've felt so helpless since the men left."

"Just organizing ourselves will help," I say. "I think the roan's getting used to you. Can you harness her and try to coax her along the furrow?"

"Of course," she says. She starts to leave, then turns back and embraces me. "I'm glad you'll stay." As she walks away, there's a bounce in her step that I haven't seen since last fall.

I'm smiling when I turn back to Eogan. "Do you need to hunt today?"

"No." He nods toward a deer carcass hanging high in a tree inside his fenced yard. "That should give us all a good meal tomorrow if we can spare youngsters to turn the spit. And everyone has grain and salmon from the stream."

"Then let's get you up to the pass to watch for trouble. I'll go along."

The rocks that tower above the trail hold passageways and nooks on both sides. One recess in the stone is larger than the others and gives a good view down onto the pass; sentries from the village have used it as shelter and lookout for generations. A cooking pot and a pile of bedskins are hidden under a ledge in the farthest corner.

"Will the women be able to stand watch?" Eogan asks.

I laugh. "Women can handle most tasks if they try."

He ducks his head sheepishly. "I guess you do everything any other warrior does."

"Aye," I say, but I think for a moment of the time I failed to do a warrior's duty.

He looks puzzled by my silence, and I hurry to go on. "The women of Enfert have always had enough work to do without attempting things that men did. Now that there is no choice, they'll watch, and they'll fight, and they will do whatever else they must. But we have no trained warriors now—except for you. It seems from your success at hunting that you can handle a spear."

"Aye. And a sword, too, if I had one." He sounds confident.

"When did you learn sword fighting?"

"When you did. I watched almost every day. I'd hurry with my chores and then hide behind the bushes near your barn. I'd watch Moren show you how to hold the sword and how to fool your opponent and switch hands. Then I'd take a piece of wood and practice by myself in the forest. I wanted to fight and ride like you and Moren."

"Show me." I take my sword out of its sheath and hand it to him, hilt first.

He hefts it for a moment to get the feel, then tosses it from hand to hand. His smile grows broader and broader as he demonstrates the footwork and thrusts of a swordsman. I pick up a piece of firewood and engage him in a mock battle. He parries my moves, ducks under my thrusts, then turns away from me and comes back with the sword in his other hand.

I toss away the firewood and reach out for my sword; he hesitates for a moment, looking down at the blade, before he hands it to me. After I replace it in its scabbard, I grasp his wrists and study them. "You need practice for endurance. Look at my wrists." I drop his hands and hold my arms out before him, turning and flexing them so that he can see the way muscles build up in a true warrior.

His smile fades. "I tried, but wood isn't very heavy."

"Of course not," I say. "You are as accomplished as my best students at Dun Alyn." I think of Sorcha and wonder where she is and what she is doing now. "I was not criticizing; I'm amazed at your ability and at the fact that you have done all of this by yourself."

His smile returns. "I'll look for heavier wood."

"Use this for a while." I slip my sword belt off and put it over his head so that it lies properly across his chest. He is taller than I am, so I adjust the belt to put the hilt in the correct position. "You have learned all that you can from sticks. You must practice now with a real sword. While you are up here on watch, you can use your time well."

I leave him holding my sword across his palms and staring at it in awe.

On the way down to the village, I ponder the problem of weapons. Another swordsman would be a help, but swords cost a great deal, and few smiths in Britain make them. I know of no one in this area who can forge anything but the plainest iron tools and spearpoints. My sword was made by the greatest sword maker in Britain at his smithy far to the east.

I stop beside our old homeplace and inhale the sharp smoke smell that still hangs in the air. A few posts stand to mark the shape of the house and the position of the barn, but everything else is gone, reduced to black ashes that rustle and turn to powder in the breeze.

I search Aten's barn and find a wooden spade. She must have their good iron-shod one at the field, but this will do. Machonna whines from the doorway, and I stop to scratch his ears. The wound is healing well, and he is no longer feverish. I let him roam around the yard for a few minutes, then close him in the house. I'm happy to hear a few mournful howls as I leave. Soon he will be able to follow me around.

When I reach the high place where Moren's and Grenna's graves lie, I see another pile of rocks atop a new patch of disturbed earth. This must be Cryner's grave. I search about the area and find a suitable stone to add to the small cairn that Jon built for him.

I sit on a sun-warmed rock, thinking of my foster mother and father. It has been less than a year since we carried Moren's body up here to lie beside Grenna's, but it seems a lifetime. I feel close to them in this spot. How I wish I could talk with them, tell them my problems, hear the advice they would give me.

"I failed to protect my chief," I say. "I was startled by the sight of Durant and froze while others pushed forward."

The only response is the gentle sound of wind in the trees on the hilltop. If Moren could hear me, I do not know what he would say. Perhaps it is just as well that I do not have to face him.

Finally I take a deep breath, shove aside the pile of stones on top of his grave, and plunge the wooden spade into the soil that covers his body. On the third stab I hit something hard and put the spade aside to scoop soil away from the spot with my hands. A dank smell of decay wafts out of the darkness, and I turn my head to gulp fresh sweet air. When I feel metal against my fingers, I grasp it carefully and tug. It catches on something, and my stomach lurches as I picture Moren's arms over the sword. I cannot avoid the stench now, and I try to hold my breath as I keep tugging and turning the blade to free it from whatever holds it in the grave.

At last the hilt breaks free, and I slide the sword out of the earth into the sunlight. A winter underground has not harmed it; there is a thin layer of rust over the iron blade, but a fine-grained stone will scour that away easily. The gold pommel shines as brightly as it did last fall when I placed it on Moren's chest.

"Forgive me, Father," I say as I smooth earth back over the mound. "I know that you give up the weapon gladly for our need. Lie in peace now and let nothing else disturb you."

I build the cairn up to its original height and stand for a few minutes thinking of the two people who lie here, and also of the good dog beside them. My tears dampen each grave before I return to the village.

I stop at the stream and wash the sword before I continue to Eogan's house. His mother, Emer, barefoot with mud caked on her legs, is carrying a bowl of wheat and a hoe from her barn. I move the wicker gate aside and enter the yard.

"Welcome to this house," she says. "I was just returning to the field to begin planting."

"I won't keep you," I say. "But if you can get something for me, I will take it to Eogan."

She focuses on the sword, and her eyes widen in fear. Of course she recognizes it; the entire village stood with me as I placed it in Moren's grave. She glances up at the cairns and back at me.

"Moren would want us to use this." I speak as firmly as I can. "It brings his strength and his blessing to our efforts."

She looks relieved. "If you are certain, then I'll not argue. Eogan will do what he thinks best anyway. Grown to a man, he has."

"Indeed he has," I agree, "and a fine man. He said the scabbard was in the barn. Would you get it for me?"

She stands her hoe against the house wall and sets the bowl carefully on a log seat beside the door. "Do you want the shield, too?"

"No. He'll not need it today."

When I approach the lookout station, I can hear Eogan stepping and leaping about the enclosure; I smile as I picture him practicing with my sword. The sounds stop as I

116

get closer, and his voice echoes out of the rocky hollow. "Who goes?"

"Ilena."

"What have you there?" He is on top of a boulder now, looking down on me.

I hold up Moren's sword. "A weapon for a warrior."

Chapter 10

One warm morning when I've been in the vale for nearly a month, I awaken to Fiona and Kenna's laughter over some task out in the yard. It is a good sound. Women of the village often laugh and joke now, and the children squeal and play as loudly as they used to.

Aten's voice interrupts them. "Hush. You'll wake Ilena. She needs her sleep."

"Aye," Kenna says. "She works hard. I don't know what we would have done without her."

"I hope she stays," Aten says. "This is her real home."

"Ilena has a life in the East, Mother," Fiona says. "She will return to it someday."

I stretch and yawn, but I don't get up at once. I need

to think about what I should do. Fiona is right. I must leave soon.

I've tried to teach my friends here how to defend themselves, and I think I have succeeded.

The women were hesitant at first. Fiona said, "I can't get used to the thought that I'm to try to kill someone." There was a murmur of agreement from the others.

"That is because you've never had to defend yourselves," I said. "Think about the day the war band came and took the men away. Would you have stabbed one of those warriors with a spear to keep your husband or your brother or son safely here with you?"

"Oh, yes," Aten answered.

Kenna's eyes widened as she looked down at her belly, and Fiona nodded vigorously.

"Then think about saving your child or your husband as you attack the straw target," I said, "and when you face an enemy, remember that they threaten you and your family."

The women train every day now, and their confidence increases with each session. All of them practice driving spears into the straw men that Eogan has hung from a low tree limb, and we've worked together in finding ways to use farm tools for defense. The children hold contests at slinging while they watch the livestock, and some have become skilled enough to bring down a rabbit or a squirrel for the family stew kettle.

I get up at last and saunter out into the yard. Kenna is

leading the roan out of the barn, and Fiona is leaving with Nessa for sentry duty. In the distance I can see Eogan and Legg headed toward the pass on a hunting trip.

"I want to exercise Rol this morning," I say. "I'll come along to the fields later."

"No need," Kenna says. "We've nearly finished plowing the last patch, and plants are coming up already in most. There should be a good crop of wheat and oats, thank the gods."

Rol has spent the past month in Aten's paddock, cropping the lush grass, though I've made sure to exercise him as often as I can. Machonna leaps around us as I fasten harness fittings and cinch down the saddle. He, too, has had a long, healing rest and seems as strong as ever now.

I ride toward the far end of the valley, where almost impassable mountains close us in. I hold Rol to a brisk trot until we pass the last house, then stop and look back at the village. Kenna has reached the fields, and Delya is helping her wrestle the heavy plow into place behind the horse. Two other women are at work pulling weeds out of a field of young oats. The children have gathered a cow and three sheep already and are proceeding along the path, collecting the rest of the livestock as they go.

When I turn Rol away from the settlement, a hare bursts out of deep grass and races ahead of us. Machonna yelps with joy and charges after it. I give Rol his head and we race across the meadow toward the mountains. The hare soon goes to ground somewhere in a gorse patch, and Rol and I go on, leaving the hound snuffling and digging his way into the bushes. We splash across a small stream and climb the first of the hills that begin the mountain range.

It feels good to be by myself and free to focus on my thoughts.

By the time Rol has climbed the second hill, he is tired, and I dismount and loosen his bit so that he can graze while I go ahead on foot along a narrow rocky path that I remember. My destination is a ledge above a quiet mountain lake. When I reach it, I sit down and lean back against the cliff behind me. I cannot see the village from here, and it seems as if I am alone in the world.

Jon and I climbed up here almost two years ago. It was the last time that we talked of marriage.

Moren had made it plain to me that I was not to tie myself to the Vale of Enfert. "Jon is a good man, Ilena," he'd said, "but you have a place outside this valley, and I cannot agree to a betrothal between you and anyone from Enfert."

I knew, of course, that my upbringing differed from that of the other young people in the vale, and it was clear that my training as a warrior would be little help to me if I became a farmer's wife. Still, I had grown up with Jon and Fiona, and I longed to go with him to the singings that all the other young people attended. I especially envied Fiona and the other girls when they paired off with the young men whom they would marry and strolled off in the evenings to be alone together.

As the two of us sat in this place, Jon asked, "Will you consider marriage?"

I hesitated, then answered, "I cannot, Jon. Moren is firm about it. I will go sometime to another place, perhaps to stay. I'm a warrior, and you do not need a warrior for a wife."

We stayed here that evening until the first star appeared above the pass, talking of our feelings and pledging to be friends forever. Then we walked back through the darkness to find Moren angrily pacing about the yard around our house.

"I'm sorry, sir," Jon said. "We walked up into the mountains at the end of the vale, and I didn't realize how late it was."

Moren looked at the two of us, and his face softened. "I understand," he said. "But you must both realize that Ilena will not stay here in the Vale of Enfert. One day we must go back."

Soon after that Jon and Kenna began walking to the singings together while I stayed at home. After Moren's death, Fiona made a plea for me to reconsider Jon's proposal, but I knew then that I must journey to the East and learn where I had come from.

I sit staring at the lake, thinking of my foster parents and my childhood here in the vale, until the sun is past midway to noon. I must get back and see if I'm needed in the fields.

Rol is still cropping grass near the spot where I left him,

and Machonna is resting in a nest of tall grass nearby. I re-place Rol's bit and lead him down the hill, with the hound following us. When we reach the small summit of the next hill, I can see down into the village.

Cattle, sheep, and goats are milling around near the last house; the youngsters are gathered on the other side of the village, near the pass. The mare stands, still harnessed to the plow, in the field, and the women are hurrying toward the children.

It is eerie to see the activity but be too far away to hear anything. There must have been an alarm. I mount and guide Rol down the hill, then urge him into a run when we reach the flat grassland.

I ride through the settlement and up the slope just in time to see a group of dark-bearded men wearing animal-skin garments and carrying short spears disappear over the pass. Two bodies lie on the trail, just outside the remains of my old homestead.

I piece the story together from the excited reports.

"We kept slinging stones, Ilena," Calum shouts. "Just like you told us to. It stopped them!"

"I felt a great anger," Aten says. "I thought of our children and knew I had to act." She carries a bloody scythe on her shoulder.

I look at the bodies on the trail and point to the one without its head. "Yours?" I ask.

She nods. "I did not think I could do it, but I did. You are right. A scythe works just like a sword. I whirled around with it like you said."

The other dead man has a spear sticking out of his chest. "Who did this?" I ask.

Kenna looks surprised and proud at the same time. "I chased him. When I got close, he turned and threatened me. I cast my spear like we'd done at the straw men. I could not believe it when he fell."

Fiona and Nessa have joined us. "They ran west along the trail," Nessa pipes. "We kept slinging stones at them as long as we could reach them."

"I doubt they'll be back," I say. The panic I felt when I realized that there was danger and that I was too far away to help has subsided. In its place is a growing awareness that my friends can defend themselves.

In late afternoon Eogan returns from hunting just as we gather around the fire in Delya's yard to talk about the day.

"I saw two bodies near the pass," he says. "What happened?" He looks at me, but Calum and Nessa answer, each vying for his attention.

"We had the livestock partway to pasture when we heard the alarm," Calum says.

"I was on sentry duty with Fiona," Nessa says. "They came sneaking along the trail—eight of them—and we waited like Ilena had told us, until they were on the pass. Then we called the alarm and started slinging stones at them."

"Let me hang the deer and put Legg away," Eogan says. "I want to hear every detail."

"I'll help you," Calum says.

When they return, the story of the battle is told all over again while I remain silent. I listen and enjoy the new confidence the women and children have gained.

As people get ready to leave Delya's yard for their homes, I say, "Machonna and I will hunt tomorrow; perhaps we can find a boar for a true victory feast."

＊ ＊ ＊

I awaken early and slip out of the house with Machonna. This will be the dog's first hunt with me since his injury, and he watches happily as I put hunting spears into the case on Rol's harness. We stop at the lookout on top of the pass to talk with Eogan.

"Come see," he says. "I kept busy last evening."

A few feet down the slope that leads to the east-west trail there is a wide tree that overhangs the path. Two human heads hang from a branch. They are easily visible to anyone coming up the trail toward the pass.

"That should slow down attackers," I say.

Eogan smiles grimly. "Aten supplied one head, and I took the other from the one killed by a slingstone. He didn't need it anymore."

"No," I agree, "he didn't."

I walk a few steps down the path to get a good view. "They serve as a good warning," I say.

"Are you going hunting?"

"Aye. I hope to find a boar to roast alongside your deer for a feast tonight."

He looks worried. "Shall I go with you? They might still be around."

"You need sleep. I'll be fine. I have Machonna now." The dog looks up at his name and howls. "I'd better go on. Your relief will be here soon. Were you alone all night?"

"Calum came up to keep me company and to talk about the battle. He's been asleep for a while."

"He did a fine job."

Eogan nods. "I think we can manage. The women are good fighters now that they know how."

The boar that Machonna and I bring back roasts in the village cooking pit all afternoon while the deer is spitted above another fire nearby. By the time the sun has fallen behind the tallest hills to the west, we have gathered to share the feast. When Eogan and Calum hoist the steaming carcass out of the pit, I step forward with my dirk in hand.

"You know from the stories that the greatest hero at a feast receives the first serving. I don't know what to do. I see heroes everywhere." There are broad smiles throughout the group.

"Calum is a hero because he led the slingers so well, but each of you"—I look from child to child—"is a hero because you were so brave, and you have become so skilled with the sling."

I look at Kenna. "Kenna is a hero because she ran, hard as it is for her at this time, and chased the invaders up the pass. Aten . . ."

There are murmurs of approval and someone says, "Aten beheaded their leader."

"I can't choose one hero out of so many, so I will serve you all in turn; let's begin with Calum and his troop of slingers."

After we have eaten and large portions have been carried up to the sentries, Eogan piles more wood on the fire against the cool evening breeze. Delya takes her place on a log seat and prepares to entertain us—no doubt with the tale of yesterday's attack.

The sentries' first calls sound like the beginning of her story, but Delya's lips are not moving, and the warning continues. A stranger on the pass.

Chapter 11

A lone horse and rider descend the path.

Eogan and I carry our swords, and others grasp spears or staffs while most of the youngsters have pouches open and slings in hand.

We meet our visitor near the remains of my home. Her travel costume is much like mine, but she wears her white hair long and loose, held back with a gold circlet. The sword hilt protruding from her harness scabbard is gold, as are the bangles on her arm. She halts her horse a few feet from us and surveys the group.

"You are prepared for an attack, it seems," she says. Her voice is strong and melodious. "I saw the warnings on the trail."

The children look at each other and grin; all of them, and most of the adults, have traveled up to the pass to see Eogan's handiwork.

She looks at each of us; it is probably my imagination that her gaze lingers on me for a time. "I am alone," she says. "I would welcome shelter for the night . . . and perhaps a bite of that roasted boar that I smell."

"We—" I stop. It is easy to forget myself; I am not the leader of this village.

Delya steps forward. "You are welcome here. We were not expecting a guest and have already eaten, but there is plenty of boar meat and also deer. I am the storyteller, and I would be honored if you stayed in my humble house." She turns to Calum. "Your father's barn is big enough for the lady's horse. Can you care for it?"

Calum nods. "Aye. Eogan will help me."

Eogan has stepped forward to hold the horse's reins with one hand and to offer his other arm to assist the woman. As she slides off her horse, I catch a glimpse of her pendant; it is a hammered copper disk with a large chunk of malachite in the center. Only a high priestess may wear malachite; it is sacred to them.

When she has dismounted, she stares at Eogan's sword before turning to face the rest of us. She speaks first to Delya. "Thank you. I am sure I will be comfortable in your home." Then she looks around. "And where are the men of the village?"

There is silence. Even though we have repelled one attack, no one wants to announce that our men and boys are not here to defend us.

At last Aten speaks. "They are gone, but we expect them soon."

She nods and says, "I am Vorgel. I am weary with traveling, and I appreciate your welcome."

Vorgel is high priestess of all Britain! Her authority equals that of Dubric, the head Druid. It is hard to believe that she has ridden unescorted into this remote settlement.

When our guest is seated in a place of honor beside the storyteller and is supplied with a large trencher of pork, Delya begins the story. She tells about the attackers of yesterday morning, describes the battle in great detail, and ends with a mention of Eogan's display on the trail. There is much about Calum and Aten. Nessa and Fiona are named, and Kenna is praised, but my name is not mentioned.

Still, I feel Vorgel's eyes on me several times during the story and so am not surprised to find her beside me when the gathering ends.

"Will you walk with me, Ilena?" she asks. "I want to see the place where you lived with Moren and Grenna."

So she does know who I am! I wonder how—and whether she knows the story of my exile. "Of course," I say. She puts her arm through mine and lets me lead her.

"You knew Moren and Grenna?" I ask.

She laughs, and the sound is a rich melody of notes. "I

130

knew your foster father when he was a babe. His mother, Gwlech, was my friend; we spent ten years together on Gorre at the school for Druids. I visited Dun Alyn often when Moren and Cara were young."

"How long have you known about me?"

"Cara told me about you when I visited Dun Alyn five years ago."

"Moren did not speak of you," I say.

"No. I've spent little time on the main isle of Britain these past years. Those in the south have forgotten their priestesses; many even live without Druids. Some of those who learned the new faith from the Romans taught their descendants to hate us. It has been safer to stay in the western isles, where we have both our own monks and our old customs."

I shake my head. I was brought up to believe in the new religion and to honor the old customs also; I don't understand why there is so much conflict.

When we reach the burned patches that held my childhood home, she looks over the devastation and then raises her eyes to the graves. The cairns that mark them are outlined against the evening sky.

"What brings you here at this time?" I ask.

She sighs. "Two reports. The first of a noble young woman driven from her rightful place by treachery and witchcraft."

I'm silent for a moment, letting her words sink in. It's

hard to imagine that a high priestess would travel across the water and venture alone on dangerous trails because of my misfortune. At last I ask, "How did you find out?"

She smiles. "News travels fast. A bard who visited Dun Dreug just as they returned from the battle at the Ford of Dee carried the story to us within a few days. Soon after, Gillis's report of his decision about your fate came to the head Druid by messenger as is proper in such grave matters."

I cannot meet her eyes. "I failed my people," I say.

"Perhaps. Still, your decision to accept the judgment due a warrior speaks for your courage. If I had had even a hint of Andrina's plans, I would have been at your side at the Ford of Dee."

"You believe that I saw Durant, then?"

She nods. "It is the kind of thing that Andrina would do. She is skilled with herbs and knows poisons that render a person senseless but still able to stand and walk."

I shudder. "Have you had any word about him?"

"No. He must have been her captive that day, and if so"—she hesitates a moment before continuing—"it is unlikely that he is still alive."

I force back a sob. "I've thought that, of course, but still I must try to find him or at least learn what has happened to him. I had hoped to travel to Dun Lachan when I left Dun Alyn, but I stopped here to leave my injured dog and found that the men of the vale had been kidnapped. I felt that I had to help my old friends."

"I heard the story of the battle with invaders. How did the women and children in this vale learn to fight?" she asks.

"They worked hard."

She laughs. "I think you must have worked also. Are you free to leave now?"

"Yes," I say. "Yesterday when the raiders from Eriu came, I was up in the mountains at the east end of the valley, and Eogan was away hunting. The women and children did a fine job of defending the village."

We stand, watching darkness creep down the mountain and fill the valley. When we turn at last to go back to the village, the path is barely visible beneath our feet. "You said two things brought you here," I say. "What is the other?"

"Arthur has disappeared."

"The Dragon Chief!" I stop on the trail and turn to her, but I cannot see her face in the darkness. The vale is quiet around us, with only the sounds of the gentle calls of birds settling into their roosts and the steady gurgle of the stream as it meanders through the village on its way to the meadow. "When?" I ask. "How? What will happen to the alliance?"

"Twelve days ago he was at his home fortress a day's journey from Uxelodunum. Many of his companions had gone to their own places for short visits before mustering for the battle that is to come. A traveler, a stranger to Arthur's hall, asked hospitality and, when pressed for news, told a story of a great boar in woods to the west. Arthur likes nothing better than a good hunt and decided to ride out the next day in search of the animal."

"Surely he took companions with him," I say.

She sighs. "Two. Only two. No one knows what happened, but none of them returned. Arthur's horse, without saddle, harness, or weapons, came home in the evening. The next morning searchers found the bodies of his companions in the area that the traveler had described, but there was no sign of Arthur."

"He should not have gone without a full war band."

She takes my arm again, and the two of us continue down the path toward the village. "Of course not," she says, "but he has hunted since he was a boy and thinks nothing of dashing out into the forest in search of a boar or stag. Arthur is young; he seems to have no fear and rarely considers his own safety."

"And the traveler?" I ask.

"Vanished. He left Arthur's fortress early in the morning after he'd told his story, and no one has seen him since, though a search went out for him as well."

"How did you receive the news?"

"Messengers come and go between Uxelodunum and Gorre constantly; it is a day's journey by sea. Dubric left at once for Uxelodunum to direct Arthur's forces there, and I set sail a few days later to travel to Dun Dreug and thence to Cameliard. The Vale of Enfert is on the trail that I take from the sea eastward, and I hoped to find you here. It seemed a likely place for you to have taken refuge."

"I'm glad that you came when you did. Otherwise we would have missed each other," I say. "I plan to leave for Dun Lachan in a day or two."

We are near Delya's house now, and Vorgel speaks quietly. "You must do something else instead."

"But . . ." I've waited too long already!

She whispers, but her words are clear and forceful. "Finding Arthur is our most important task."

Delya approaches, and we fall silent.

"Your bed is ready, lady, and a basin of warm water."

"Thank you," Vorgel says. "That sounds wonderful." She turns to me. "We will leave soon after sunup tomorrow. We can talk as we travel."

I lie awake long after Aten, Fiona, and Kenna have fallen asleep, my mind churning with worry about Durant. I know it will be hard to tell Vorgel that I cannot carry out whatever task she has for me, but I must find the words. Durant is my betrothed; I have a duty to him. There are probably hundreds searching for Arthur; one more person cannot be important. I vow to be firm when I speak with her tomorrow.

When I awaken, I am distressed to find that it is well past sunup. Then I feel relief. Vorgel has gone. Perhaps she left in anger because I did not appear. But at least I have been spared the struggle of refusing to do what the high priestess ordered.

I wander out into the bright morning and find Aten baking bannocks at the outside fire. "You slept soundly at last," she says. "I told our visitor that you had a restless night."

"I'm sorry that I missed her," I say.

Aten stands to hand me a small hot loaf and then points up the path. Vorgel is near my old homeplace; she has one hand on her horse's withers, and she is pointing toward the south with the other one. Eogan is beside her, nodding as he listens.

Suddenly I lose my appetite. I hand the bread back to Aten and start up the path.

Machonna dashes past me and butts his head against Eogan's knee, demanding attention. Eogan scratches the hound's ears, but keeps his eyes on Vorgel.

"It is a good day to travel, Ilena," she says as I approach.

"Yes," I say. "I wish you Godspeed."

Her eyes twinkle for a moment, but she speaks sternly. "Our paths run together for a half day's travel. I will leave you at the north-south trail."

I struggle for words. "I . . . I must look for Durant. He is my betrothed, and I cannot leave him to whatever danger he's in."

"Eogan will travel with you to the South," she says.

I look at Eogan. He is trying to appear calm and unconcerned, but excitement sparkles in his eyes. "Eogan is not free to travel anywhere," I protest. "The village needs him; his mother will not want him to leave."

"She told me to do as the lady commands," he says. "She is preparing my pack and food for both of us; Fiona and Kenna are harnessing our horses."

Anger overcomes me, and I turn to Vorgel. "You cannot—" Morning sun glints for a moment on the malachite necklace. No one, not even a chief, tells a high priestess what she may or may not do.

She waits calmly while I struggle. I think that I can even see sympathy in her eyes, but she does not speak.

Finally I say, "Tell me what we must do."

"First we will hear Eogan's pledge to you," she says. She turns to him. "Do you know the great oath?"

"The bards have talked of it," he says. "I do not know the words."

"Then repeat them after me," she says. "Heaven is above me."

Eogan's voice is clear and more grown-up than I've ever heard it. "Heaven is above me."

"And the earth is beneath me."

"And the earth is beneath me."

I listen as she speaks each line and he repeats it after her. I remember standing with Durant last fall as we pledged our loyalty to Arthur. When Eogan speaks the last line, "I will stand with Ilena," I think of what my pledge to the Dragon Chief means.

Vorgel says, "Now be quick, both of you. I'll wait for you on the other side of the pass."

Our good-byes are easier than I expected. I pull a handful of gold bangles from my pack and press them on Aten. "Take these into the nearby valleys to bargain for oxen and other livestock. Get more spearpoints, too, and a dirk for Calum."

She starts to protest, but I cut her off with a hug. "It will make my leaving easier if I know that you have some resources to help you until the men are safely home."

She smiles and returns my embrace. "Go with your God, Ilena. And come back to us when you can."

Emer has tears in her eyes, but she beams with pride in her son's new role as my companion and protector. "Godspeed to you both, and, Eogan, be strong in your duty to Ilena and to the lady Vorgel. Your father will be honored when he hears of your position."

Eogan nods solemnly and says, "Greet my father for me when you see him." He embraces Emer and takes Legg's rein from Kenna.

Fiona clasps my hand tightly for a moment, then steps back and hands me Rol's rein.

I thought at first to leave Machonna behind; he is happy here, and Aten loves him. But I know that he would follow us as soon as he was free to roam, and to be truthful, I enjoy his company. My life has had too many losses lately. I put his collar and leash on top of Rol's pack and let the hound run beside us as we lead the horses up the pass.

We stop near the top and turn to look down on the village. Everyone is still standing beside the path, where they gathered to wish us well. Eogan and I wave and watch for a moment, then trudge on, with Legg and Rol following and Machonna leading the way.

Calum is on watch with his mother; both come down from their rocky hideaway to speak with us. "The lady met someone. He was waiting just on the other side of the pass, but we didn't even know he was near," Calum says.

"Aye. A proper old hermit, he looked," his mother adds.

And a proper old hermit he does appear when we see him near the bottom of the incline. His clothing is a tattered cloak over a skin garment; his feet are bare, and his long, graying hair falls from a Druid tonsure that exposes his forehead and a clean-shaven patch of scalp across the front of his head. He wears a short sword and carries a hunting bow. A quiver of arrows is slung on his back and more are bundled onto a pack on his donkey. The animal looks much like his master, shaggy and well past the prime of his life.

"Arno," Vorgel says, and makes no further explanation for him.

He nods and moves ahead of us, tugging his donkey along by a thin frayed rope.

Vorgel leads her horse too, and she and I walk together.

Eogan falls into place behind us, and Machonna bounds beside him, stopping often to sniff at promising spots along the path, then racing to catch up. Arno swings his head from side to side, surveying the trail ahead and the forest on either side as efficiently as any scout I've watched. When I look back at Eogan, I note that he has taken his cue from the hermit and guards us from the rear.

My companion does not start a conversation, so I too remain silent.

At a little past noon Arno stops us at a clearing; it is a place with a spring and rock outcroppings where Moren and I often rested on our hunting trips. Vorgel goes at once to a ledge near the spring and sits down with her back against the rock face. Eogan and I water the horses and the donkey at the small stream that flows from the spring, while Arno and Machonna disappear into the woods around us. They return as I am dipping fresh water for Vorgel.

She takes a long drink before she speaks. "Is anyone around?"

"No one that I can spot," Arno answers. "And the dog didn't sense anything."

"Good. We'll rest and talk for a time. Bring us meat and bread from my pack, Ilena. You and Eogan must save your provisions for your journey. Arno and I will be at Dun Dreug late tonight."

I obey, carrying dried meat strips and a barley loaf to her. Arno takes a barley loaf and heads across the clearing to a fallen tree trunk; Eogan scoops up a loaf and several strips of meat, then joins him. Machonna gulps down a meat strip, then drops to the ground at my feet and is soon asleep.

When Vorgel and I have finished our food, she says, "I wish that I could keep you with me, but we must separate for a few days. The task that I have for you should not be dangerous if you are careful."

Eogan has stretched out on the tree trunk and seems to be asleep; Arno has disappeared into the forest again. Vorgel stands and paces back and forth for a few steps, then sits back down. "We know that Saxons and those who support them plan to attack Cameliard."

My lessons with Moren were clear about Cameliard. It is situated above the river Forth, and the fortress controls the eastern approaches to North Britain just as Alcluith controls River Clota with its sea access from the west.

She continues. "The battle challenge that Faolan issued to Dun Alyn was part of a plan to defeat the four northern fortresses that are loyal to Arthur—Dun Alyn, Dun Dreug, Dun Selig, and Glein.

"Faolan and Andrina's failure to win that battle was a setback; however, the plan to attack Cameliard has gone forward as they planned. Saxons from the South of Britain, and those northern tribes who oppose Arthur's alliance, stream toward their muster at Alcluith.

"Dubric's messengers have hurried through Britain the past month, alerting all members of Arthur's alliance. In addition, I've sent word to Belert, Perr, Lenora, and Doldalf to meet with me tomorrow at Dun Dreug. Then they will lead their war bands to Cameliard to await the attack there."

"But what about Arthur?" I ask.

"We will be sorely weakened at Cameliard without his leadership. If he is not restored to us, I fear for the entire alliance."

"Nothing would stop the Saxon tribes then," I say.

"True. They hold the South of Britain already; they've formed alliances with tribes of the Far North. Only Arthur and those loyal to him stop them from controlling the central part of the isle. Nothing is more important than Arthur's presence at Cameliard."

She is right. My concern about Durant and my work with my people in Enfert had driven thoughts of the danger to Britain from my mind. "I apologize for lagging this morning," I say. "I had lost sight of my duties to Arthur."

And to Dun Alyn. If my people are going into battle, I must be with them. Even if I am not a chief, if I must walk with the spear carriers or the slingers, my place is with Belert and our warriors.

"You were focused on two important tasks," she says. "You did wonders at leading the people of Enfert to mount their own defense; your concern for Durant is proper, and your plan to ride north to search for him was wise though dangerous. However, you must lay those thoughts aside now and undertake this task.

"I will leave Dun Dreug as soon as I've met with the chiefs and lead a small band toward Alcluith. You know the situation there?"

I nod. Alcluith is an ancient fortress of Britain, but it came under Saxon control three years ago. Its loss was a devastating blow to our people. Andrina's sister, Camilla, rules it now with her Saxon husband.

She continues. "Dubric and I believe that Arthur must be a captive there—if he is still alive. It is the safest prison in Britain, and only a few days' travel from the place he was captured."

"Can we get into the fortress?"

"You are not to try. Your job is to see how many war bands have gathered around it. Groups have been moving into the area for days. Knowing where the camps are will help us plan how to get into the fortress to search for Arthur, and it will tell us how many warriors are assembling for the coming battle at Cameliard."

Arno has appeared at Vorgel's side, and Eogan is stretching after his nap. Machonna rouses himself and wanders around the clearing, sniffing at rocks and trees.

Vorgel takes a stick and breaks off a few slivers to make a sharp point. "Watch now, all three of you. Arno, you must be sure I am accurate. Eogan and Ilena, memorize this so that you know your route and where to meet me."

She swipes leaves and grass from a spot beside the spring and pats the mud smooth before she begins to scratch lines in it. "We are here, and this is the trail to the south. It will take you three more days to reach a spot opposite Alcluith where you can see the enemy camps."

Her instructions make it sound simple enough. We will go south on the main trail until we reach a long lake, where we will continue along the west side of the water. The lake drains into a river called Leven, and River Leven meets River Clota a half day's journey to the south. We are to note the ford that lies a little south of the lake, but we are to pass it without crossing and climb a hill to observe the area around Alcluith.

"Alcluith is here," she says. She places a small stone at the point where the east bank of River Leven meets the north bank of Clota. "It is an island."

"But we'll be on the west bank of Leven and it must widen as it meets Clota," I say. "How do we get across to Alcluith?"

"You don't! Your goal is not to reach the fortress but to observe it from the far bank. There are hills that will give you a vantage point." Her stick jabs the earth along the west bank of Leven where it approaches Clota. "You should reach a suitable place by twilight three days from now—if all goes well."

I do not like the worried look on her face. "What can go wrong?"

"It is dangerous for you to be near Alcluith. But we expect the battle at Cameliard to begin in six or seven days, so

I need information as soon as possible. We must try to free Arthur—if it is not too late."

Eogan continues to stare at the drawing. He points to the Ford of Leven. "I'd think the greatest danger would be here, then."

"Exactly," Vorgel says. "Though you could encounter hostile war bands anywhere." She drags her foot over the drawing until it is wiped out. "Now, let us be going."

As we move steadily eastward, my mind swirls with thoughts of Dun Alyn. If my people are to meet Vorgel at Dun Dreug tomorrow night, they must be on the trail now. I long to be with them, and the pain of my exile is almost more than I can bear.

The north-south trail is wider than the track we've followed from the Vale of Enfert, and the center portion is worn down by the generations of travelers that have walked and ridden along it. We stop for a few minutes to rest and to say our good-byes; then Vorgel and Arno continue east toward Dun Dreug, and Eogan and I turn south toward Alcluith.

Chapter 12

We get our first look at the lake the next morning. It is a cold, wet journey southward on a narrow trail along the western shore as we camp under damp tree cover at night and trudge through mud and over slippery rocks during the day. We finally see the south shore of the lake in the distance on the third evening after we leave Vorgel. It is getting dark, so we make camp in a small forested glen. I'm so tired from traveling over the rough terrain that I sleep soundly all night.

When I awaken, the sun is bright behind the mountains across the water. Eogan is harnessing the horses, and Machonna is gnawing on a hard piece of bread. From my sleeping place I have a good view of the lake below us.

Someone is rowing a leather boat toward shore, and I watch the small craft bob up and down as the paddle dips into the water first on one side and then on the other. Finally I pull my attention away from the peaceful scene and think of our instructions.

"We should have left long ago," I grumble as I stand and stretch. "We must reach the viewpoint that Vorgel described well before dark today."

"I'm sorry." Eogan yawns as he speaks. "I slept too late."

"We are both tired," I say. "I should have awakened sooner myself."

We are leading the horses out of the trees when Machonna growls. He stands near the trail and stares to his left. The hair on his back rises, and he growls again.

I hand Rol's rein to Eogan and point back into the trees, then race for Machonna. He balks, but I manage to drag him up past our sleeping spot into the deep tree cover and pull his leash from my pack.

"What is it?" Eogan whispers.

I shake my head. "I wasn't close enough to the trail to see. Be still and listen."

For a moment the only sound is Machonna's low growl, but soon we hear horses. I keep my eyes on a gap in the trees that shows a sliver of the trail below us. A horseman appears, followed by three others. All four are heavily armed, and they ride at a brisk pace.

"Only four," Eogan whispers, "but it's well that we are not ahead of them."

"Those could be scouts," I say. "There may be a war band behind them."

Machonna has not relaxed; he continues to strain against the leash and growl. It is only a few moments before we hear horses again. I do not recognize the first two people who pass, but the third is unmistakable. The vividly colored hair, the chestnut mustache, and the wolfskin cloak are all familiar. It is Faolan, and Sorcha rides behind him.

I draw in my breath so sharply that Eogan turns to look at me. "You recognize them?" he whispers.

I nod. My anger grows with each warrior that I see below us.

The sun has risen well above the mountain by the time the last of Faolan's followers has gone by.

As soon as they are out of sight, Eogan asks, "Who are they?"

"My enemies!" I answer.

"What should we do?" he asks.

"Wait. It is all that we can do. Since their destination must be Alcluith or a mustering ground near it, they will have to cross the Ford of Leven, and it will take a troop that size quite a while. We'll give them a good head start before we attempt the trail."

Eogan loosens the horses' bits so that they can graze, and I tie Machonna securely.

"How far is the ford?" he asks.

"Less than a half day's travel, I think."

"And we must go some distance past it, climb a steep hill to observe the countryside, and return to the ford in time to meet Vorgel tomorrow morning. Is that possible?"

"Aye." I try to sound more cheerful than I feel. "Vorgel and her war band will wait until we arrive."

He shakes his head. "What if . . ."

"Stop worrying," I snap. "We'll push on as soon as we can. Now get some rest!"

He glares at me and stomps to the bed of pine branches he slept on last night.

I feel a pang of guilt for being so sharp, but I'm worried about accomplishing our task too. It doesn't help to talk about how difficult it is. Eogan falls asleep at once; I stare into space and think about Faolan and Sorcha.

When the sun is almost overhead, I wake Eogan. "We must risk traveling. If they kept their pace, they should all be across River Leven by the time we get there."

The horses are refreshed from the extra rest this morning and make good time through the afternoon. I keep Machonna on the leash for a while, but release him when the trail becomes too narrow for him to walk beside Rol.

We reach the ford before the light has faded; the summer solstice is so close that nights now are completely dark for only a short time between the last glow of twilight and the first glimpse of dawn.

Machonna races up and down the riverbank, sniffing and whimpering; he looks across the water and back at me to see if we are going to cross. I dismount and pull him to me to fasten the leash.

"How far ahead of us are they?" I ask.

Eogan dismounts and stoops down, studying the tracks closest to the water. "It looks like these"—he points to a pair of footprints so sharp that I can see each toe outlined separately—"were just made. See how they are blurring as the water laps at them?"

I look across the ford at the shrubs and trees on the other side of the river. Any number of Dun Struan warriors could be watching us at this moment. The skin on my scalp prickles, and I am aware of how exposed we are. "Let's hurry on. It's getting late, and we must find shelter."

We continue a short distance past the ford until we see a tiny stream that cuts between the steep hills, and we follow it to a clearing large enough for the animals and ourselves, but well hidden by brambles and low-hanging pines.

"Make camp," I say, "but do not risk a fire. Tie Machonna. I'll be back shortly."

"Where are you going?"

I point to a hilltop outlined against the pink and gray sky. "I'll see what is visible from that summit. Perhaps I can see Alcluith and the river Clota from here. The night campfires will tell me what I need to know."

"This isn't where Vorgel said to look."

"She told us to find out how many war bands have camped near Alcluith. We don't have time to get closer."

"Vorgel told me to stay with you."

"No, Eogan. You will remain here. Someone must care for the animals. I'll return tonight if I can; if not, I'll come in the morning."

"If you come back! I took an oath to protect you."

"You took an oath of loyalty, and that means you are to help me carry out my duty. If I do not come, be at the ford tomorrow to meet Vorgel." I pull my waterskin from Rol's harness, and a loaf of bread and some meat strips from my pack, then turn toward the stream.

"Your sword! You've forgotten your sword."

"I can't carry it through the brambles and rocks." I hesitate, then say, "Don't worry. I'll be fine." His frown remains as I clasp his hand in farewell and hurry out of the clearing.

I climb steadily alongside the little stream; by the time I've finished my bread loaf and meat strips, I've reached its source. I rest against the cliff where water drains out of the layers of rock. The sky is still streaked with pink in the west, and the light is brighter here above the glen. I test the water gushing from a large crack in the stones near me and find it sweet to the taste. I empty my waterskin and refill it with fresh cold water, then begin my climb to the summit.

A path winds its way upward, leading me around boulders and past clusters of gorse, so I move quickly with little problem despite the failing light. As I approach the final ascent to the summit, the western sky has darkened, but a nearly full moon is riding just above the hills across the river Leven to the east. When I come out at last on the top, I'm well above tree cover, and I can see to the horizon in all directions.

I turn slowly in a circle. There is nothing but darkness to the north and west. To the south I can see the river Clota; it's a bright moonlit strip that widens toward the western sea and disappears behind dark hills to the east.

Alcluith is a massive twin-peaked hulk looming up where the Leven opens into Clota. Moonlight gleams on the water around it, and there is an orange glow from fires between the two peaks.

Campfires also burn along both banks of River Clota and cluster around Alcluith, stretching back like the legs of an ungainly spider into the hills beyond the fortress. The camps line the east bank of Leven from the great fortress to a point almost opposite where I stand. I try to count them all, but give up after numbering thirty just along River Leven. There must be well over one hundred camps.

One hundred war bands of Saxons and Northerners gathered to march against Cameliard! No wonder Vorgel wanted information. There is no way to get near Alcluith without going through enemy camps.

A chill wind has risen, and it startles me. I cannot see or hear anyone near the summit, but the evening insect song has lessened. I want to get off this exposed place as soon as possible and take refuge under cover of trees or shrubs. I head down the side of the mountain, but after only a few steps, I see that I am not on the path that led me up here, and so I return to the top.

I force myself to remain calm and turn slowly until I think I see the right path. Halfway down this well-worn trail, I realize it is not my original route either. If I'm going the wrong way, I could end up hours away from our campsite. I stop and try to gain a sense of where I am. I peer out through trees and can see water stretching off in both directions. I must be heading toward River Leven, so I can take the main trail along the river back to Eogan.

I sigh with relief and try to hurry, but I'm exhausted and find myself stumbling. At last I stop just above the river and lean against a boulder, drawing in big gulps of air. As I step onto the trail, I hear a horse stamp its foot. I take two cautious steps and shrink against a tree trunk, motionless, breathing as quietly as possible, but it is too late.

"There! By the tree," a man says. "Light a torch."

I leap away from the tree and race along the path, praying that they will not bother to chase me, but I manage only a short distance before I trip and fall over a tree root. When I pick myself up, I'm in the center of a group of warriors— two women, one holding a torch, and three men, all carrying the square shields of those from north of Dee. My hand has fallen to my dirk, but strong arms drag me to my feet.

At first I twist and kick in an attempt to get free, but the men holding me are too strong. I won't give my captors the satisfaction of subduing me, so I stand still, my head high, my mouth firmly closed, and make no further resistance.

A man who seems to be the leader pulls my dirk from my belt and holds it up under my chin.

"Careful, Hana." The woman with the torch moves nearer and peers into my face. "I recognize her," she says. "I was with the scouts at the Ford of Dee. This one stood with the Druid to rouse the ones we fought. She battled like a she-devil at the end."

Hana grins and lowers the blade. He says, "Let's get across the ford and on to Alcluith then. Andrina and Faolan will want to see her." He shoves me toward the river.

A chill runs through my body. I'm to meet Andrina and Faolan again. Sorcha, too, no doubt. And now I'm an unarmed captive.

Chapter 13

Our progress is hampered by camps that have been set up on every piece of flat land along the east bank of Leven. In most cases we skirt the groups, but sometimes we must ride between clumps of warriors and their fires, which causes considerable grumbling from those near our path. My captors ignore the remarks, and no one challenges them.

I'm wedged in front of one of the women, who grips me with her brawny arms as she handles the reins. Even if I could struggle free of her, I could not get away from the rest. I twist my hands into the horse's mane and hold on with my knees.

The river widens as we approach Alcluith, and the fortress looms larger and larger.

I'm glad to slide off the horse when we stop at a channel

directly across from the fortress, but my relief quickly turns to distress when I realize I'm being dragged into a boat. The long wooden craft holds the six of us and two young men who use poles to push it over the water. While it does not bob up and down like the little leather currach I saw on the lake this morning, the sensation of moving with no good earth beneath me makes my stomach tremble.

We are poled across the channel to a narrow beach beneath the cliff. My captor drags me out of the boat with her and hurries me along with the others till we round a rocky outcrop and approach a group of warriors seated in front of a building.

A woman stands and challenges us. "And you're with Faolan's band?"

"Aye, I'm Hana of Dun Struan," the leader answers. "We're expected—up above."

I try to hold myself proudly, though I'm exhausted and every spot in my body aches. The sentry stares at me for a few moments.

"A prisoner for Faolan and Andrina," Hana says. "They'll be glad to see her."

The woman nods, and we pass behind the building and begin climbing toward the activity above us. I find it difficult to keep my balance on the rough terrain, but my captor yanks me up when I stumble.

At the narrowest point in the climb, where the cliffs

on both sides press in against the path, we meet a group coming down.

"Make way. Make way."

I freeze at the familiar voice and strain to see the speaker.

"Hurry up. They'll be wanting more wine any moment, and it'll go hard on us if we haven't got it." It is Jon, my old friend from Enfert.

I try to see if any of the others are from the vale, but most carry jugs on the shoulder closest to me so that I cannot see their faces.

I shrink against the rock to let the procession pass. My captors have let go of my arms and are so busy cursing and complaining about the delay that they aren't paying attention to me. When Jon comes level with me, I speak quietly. "Jon. Jon, is it you?"

He is watching the trail in front of him until he hears my voice. Then his head snaps up, and he stares straight at me. I see his eyes widen in shock, and his mouth opens as if he might speak, but he looks away quickly and says nothing until he is well past me.

"Move along! We have to be back up here with full wine jugs before the flagons run dry." His voice is harsher than I've ever heard it. I watch as long as I can see him, but he does not look back.

For a wild moment I am encouraged by Jon's presence; then I realize that he and any others from Enfert with him

157

must be slaves here and could not possibly help me. And I cannot help them either.

When we stagger up the last rocky patch, we are on a flat space between the two high peaks of Alcluith. A round house stands against the eastern peak, and another, rectangular in the manner of Saxon buildings, is beside it. The smell of food fills the air and servants hurry through the area with planks of meat and large wine jugs.

The ground is covered with people; at least eight fires have circles of men and women crowded together around them eating and drinking. We weave our way through, stopping now and then for my captors to exchange greetings with friends, until we are in front of the rectangular building, facing three people seated on a bench—Andrina, Faolan, and Sorcha.

Andrina lounges at one end of the wooden seat with her back against the daub wall of the building behind her. Sorcha and Faolan sit close together a short distance from her. Hana bends to speak with Faolan. I can't hear what they are saying, but Faolan smiles broadly as he listens.

I knew that I would be presented to Faolan and Andrina as a prize by my captors, and I had seen Sorcha riding with Faolan. Still, I'm not prepared for the rage that overcomes me at the sight of them. I square my shoulders, raise my head high, and clench my fists.

"Ilena!" Sorcha squeals in her excitement. "The chief of Dun Alyn herself!"

"Not chief anymore, we've heard," Faolan says. "Not that it would matter. After we take Cameliard, Dun Alyn will be next, and Sorcha will be restored as the rightful chief."

"At least I'm not a traitor to Britain!" I say as loudly as I can.

Andrina stands and looks out over the crowd. It is so quiet now that I can hear wood crackling in a nearby fire. "Welcome, friends," she begins. "We have an unexpected guest—Ilena of Dun Alyn. Once chief of that fortress, till she failed to hold her place at Belert's sword side."

There is a wave of conversation behind me.

Faolan is beside Andrina now, and when it's quiet again, he says, "A band of my scouts stumbled over Ilena near the Ford of Leven. She was alone—as befits a coward who has been forced out of her fortress." He turns to Andrina. "Will you bring out that pet of yours? And the famous Dragon Chief? We have three captives now for the ceremonies tomorrow."

Andrina's pet? Could it be Durant? Might he still be alive? My hopes rise—then crash as I realize I can't help him. The Dragon Chief, of course, is Arthur. Vorgel was right; he is a captive here. Andrina motions to someone in the crowd behind me, and four warriors come forward.

"Bring the prisoners here."

My captors have moved back into the crowd, so I am standing alone now, but I make no effort to go anywhere. I want to be right here when Arthur and Durant come—if it is

Durant. Escaping from this spot would do little good anyway. Even if I could get away from all these people, I'd still be trapped on an island.

Andrina leans over to talk with Faolan and Sorcha. I can't hear the conversation because the noise behind me has risen.

"Server! Over here!"

"Wine! Where are those wine carriers?"

"Bring more bread—and hurry with it."

Jon must be back there somewhere with his wine jug. I wish that I dared turn around to see, but I don't want to call attention to myself and risk getting tied up or removed before the other prisoners are brought.

When I hear footsteps in the darkness behind the building, I try to prepare myself for whatever happens.

The first prisoner must be Arthur. I've not seen him before, but the tall young man with red hair who strides into view, defiant despite his bound arms, matches the bards' descriptions of the Dragon Chief.

I stare into the darkness behind him, willing away my desire to see Durant and praying that he is somewhere else—somewhere safe.

But it is Durant. He is not bound. His head droops, and he seems frail. He moves listlessly and appears to have little interest in his surroundings.

"Durant!" I close the distance between us in two quick steps.

He does not respond at first. Then he looks closely at me and his face changes. "Ilena!" His arms circle my body, and we embrace for a brief sweet moment.

Rough hands tear us apart. I'm wrestled into place beside Arthur, and Hana stands near me with his hand on his sword.

Durant is pushed to a spot on Arthur's other side.

Arthur looks from one of us to the other. "Courage, friends," he says.

"Silence!" Andrina orders.

She looks out over the assembly. "Tomorrow the chiefs of Alcluith—Camilla, my sister, and Cedric, her Saxon husband—will lead us into battle. Only Cameliard stands between us and victory across the North. Dun Alyn, Dun Dreug, Dun Selig, and Glein will fall like ancient trees in a storm as we march northward. With Arthur our captive, his forces cannot hold against us.

"Tomorrow we will meet here again, and Ilena of Dun Alyn, Durant of Hadel, and Arthur himself, our captive since the last new moon, will die." She pauses for a moment and cheering breaks out. When it quiets down, she continues. "The next day they will ride with us—their heads on our spears—to lead the way to our victory."

A cold fear starts in my belly. So this is how it is to be—a sword stroke, and my head mounted on a lance to frighten my people! I take a deep breath and try to compose myself. If I'm to die, I will look courageous to the end.

"Take them away." Andrina reaches over and pushes me.

As I catch myself, I turn and find Durant watching me with such intensity that it brings tears to my eyes. A Saxon warrior holds a spear in front of him to prevent any attempt to come to me.

"Wait!" Faolan grabs my arm. His face is red from too much wine, and he slurs his words. "This woman insulted me, as her father and her sister insulted me before." He pulls his dirk from his belt and holds the blade against my cheek.

I stand very still, barely breathing, and try to keep my face expressionless.

Sorcha leans forward and says, "She killed my grandfather and forced me out of my home."

Faolan taps my face with the blade. "I'll have your revenge, Sorcha. After tomorrow no one will dispute your place as chief of Dun Alyn."

I press my lips together and force myself to keep still.

Arthur has moved from my side to a spot behind me. Now he tries to push himself between us. "Let her go, Faolan! She's no threat to you now."

Andrina signals and two warriors leap forward to pull the Dragon Chief away from us. They shove him against the building and stay beside him.

There is little I can do with a knife to my face, but I'll gain nothing by submitting helplessly to whatever torture Faolan plans. When he lowers the knife and pulls me closer to him, I gather all my strength, twist my body, and slam my knee into his groin. As he doubles over in pain, the knife flies out of his grasp and clatters onto the hard ground.

He straightens, grabs me by the hair, and slaps me across the face. The blow is so hard that I cry out despite my resolve to remain quiet.

"Let her go!" The wild cry startles everyone into silence.

Durant slams the Saxon's spear aside, scoops up Faolan's dirk, and leaps onto his back. Before he can be pulled away, he clamps his arm around the wolf-man's neck, and stabs him over and over.

The two of them lurch back and forth and stumble against me. I fall to the ground and warm blood spurts over me as I twist and roll myself out from under their feet. When I lift my head, Sorcha is moving toward us.

She holds a sword high, waiting her chance.

"Durant!" I scream as loudly as I can. "Behind you— Sorcha!" But it's too late, and I cannot get up in time to stop her.

She plunges the blade into Durant's back.

Both men, locked in a deadly embrace, fall to the ground and roll toward me. With help from Andrina, Faolan staggers to his feet, though blood is pouring from wounds in his chest.

Durant quivers and jerks on the stony ground and then lies still with the sword protruding from his back. I crawl to him and call, "Durant. Durant," but there is no response.

Chapter 14

I'm not sure how I make my way to the prison. My guards have a tight hold on my arms and carry or drag me when my legs give way. Tears are streaming down my face, and I can't wipe them away, nor do I want to.

Arthur and I are taken behind the buildings to an enclosure built against a steep cliff on what I think is the northern side of the island. There is a roofed room for guards; the two on duty are playing knucklebones when we enter.

One asks, "What happened to the other one?"

"You're rid of him, but here's a new one we picked up for you."

Both guards stare at me for a moment, then turn back to

their game. An opening at the back of the room leads to a narrow passage in the cliff. A few feet in, a space has been closed off with a wall made of bones and mortar. I can see enough by the flickering torchlight to recognize human bones, and I shudder.

Our escorts pull open a door made of the same bone and mortar mix and shove us inside. After they leave with their torch, a glow from the guardroom shows through cracks in the door. The only sounds are the rattle of the game pieces and an occasional curse or laugh from one of the guards.

Arthur has slid to a sitting position on the floor, and I sit beside him. "What can we do?" I ask.

"I don't know," he says.

"You're the Dragon Chief!" I say. "You must have some plan."

He's silent for a moment, then says wearily, "I'm not a wizard, Ilena. I wish I were."

I've tried to stop crying with no success and now the sobs come fast and hard. When I finally get some control over myself, I apologize. "I'm sorry, sir. I know you can't perform miracles. Losing Durant is more than I can bear."

"He loved you so much," Arthur says. "He was with us at Uxelodunum in the spring, before he left for Dun Alyn. All he could talk about was you."

I start sobbing again.

He sighs. "I would have done anything to save him. Durant was my cousin and my closest friend. He has ridden at my sword side ever since we were old enough to go to battle."

I've become accustomed to the dim light that creeps into the cell from the guardroom and can see Arthur leaning awkwardly against the wall. I realize that his arms are still bound, and that he looks terribly uncomfortable. "If you'd like, I'll try to untie you," I say.

He twists so that I can reach his wrists. "That would be most welcome. I've been bound most of today."

"How did you end up here?" I ask.

"They captured me not a half day's ride from my home; I had thought to have a bit of boar hunting before the muster to leave for Cameliard." He sighs. "Alpin and Uisdean were with me. Gone now, both of them. An ambush—and probably the whole story about a great boar was part of it, though I'll never trace it back."

I've managed to get one of the knots undone and move to a second one. "Was . . ." I don't even want to say his name for the pain it will bring, but I must know what happened to him. ". . . Durant here with you?"

"Aye." He pauses. "The Walking Dead, they call them. Few know the herbs for that now, and fewer still will do that to a man. Andrina may be the last of her kind. He remembered some things, but wasn't sure about a lot."

"If I had not cried out, he would be beside us now."

"You gave him the greatest gift a warrior can have. I saw my old friend in the moment when he leaped on Faolan."

"What gift?" I ask. "I caused his death!"

"You gave him life. The only life that matters to a warrior. The bards will sing of his brave attack on Faolan, and his son will hear stories of Durant as a hero. You and I will die as sacrifices before the battle tomorrow. Our heads will grieve our friends, but no one will sing of our brave deeds as we died."

I release the second knot and pull the thongs from his wrists.

"Ahhh." He moves away from me, and I can see his arms swinging slowly back and forth. "Now I can get some rest."

"I don't know what help it will be to feel rested tomorrow."

"No." His laugh has a bitter edge. "It makes no difference, I'm sure. But still one always hopes. My war bands have certainly been searching for me. I've tried this door, but it's barred on the outside, and we're never without guards."

"I don't suppose we could get off the fortress even if we got out of here," I say.

"Well, no, probably not. But we are near the north entrance here, and it's not as busy as the south one. I'd try for sure."

"Vorgel said you must be on Alcluith."

"Vorgel? Vorgel is on the mainland?"

"She came through the Vale of Enfert four days ago on her way to mobilize the northern fortresses. She sent me here to gather information and bring it to a rendezvous at the Ford of Leven."

"When will she be there?"

I think for a moment. The past few hours seem an eternity, though I know that I left Eogan only a short time ago. "Today sometime—it is surely past midnight—she and others will wait for me and my companion at the ford."

"Your companion?"

"Eogan of Enfert. A lad who thought it good to pledge his loyalty to me." I can hear the despair in my voice.

"We are chiefs, Ilena; leading people is our duty, just as dying with courage will be our duty tomorrow."

There is a commotion in the guardroom. One of the guards demands, "Who are you and what do you want?"

"I was told to bring wine to the guards. Do you want it?" It's Jon!

"Who told you? No one ever sent us wine before. A bit of ale, and watered already at that, but wine?"

"Leave it here," the other guard says. "We deserve our share."

"And if we're found tomorrow with a jar?" the first guard asks.

"I'll come back for it," Jon says. "It's worth my life to lose one, empty or full."

He must know I'm here!

"It's Jon," I whisper to Arthur. "My old friend from En-fert. I saw him earlier as they brought me in. He and the men of Enfert were carried off as slaves over a month ago."

"Perhaps there is hope," Arthur says.

The two of us sit in silence, straining to hear what is happening in the guardroom.

The only sounds are the knucklebones clanking as they're shaken and an occasional gurgling of liquid from a narrow-necked jar. Finally even those cease, and I can hear snores.

I'm starting to doze off myself when light from a small torch gleams in the passage, and Jon stands outside the bone and mortar wall.

"Can you hold this door steady while I pull off the bars?" he asks. "I don't want to make too much noise, though I think those two will sleep till tomorrow with no trouble." He settles the torch into a wall holder just across from the cell.

Arthur is ahead of me and braces the door in place while Jon lifts the two bars and places them on the floor of the passage. The men lift the door and prop it against the wall inside the cell.

Jon turns to Arthur. "You're the one they call the Dragon Chief?" he asks.

Arthur nods. "Aye, that's one thing I'm called."

"I've come for Ilena. The others are waiting with a boat." He looks at me. "He's to come too, I suppose?"

"Yes," I say. "We need him; Britain needs him. Are all of you from Enfert here?"

"No," he says. "Just Nol, Craig, and I. The others are at a place called Dun Lachan."

I nod. "We thought so."

"How did you know anything about it?"

"I've been at Enfert the past month."

"You have? How are they?"

"Well," I say. "Planting is done. Slave raiders came, but your mother, Kenna, and the others chased them away."

I can see his amazed expression even in this dim light.

Arthur interrupts. "Are we getting out of here, Jon?"

"Yes, sir. We hope so." Jon disappears into the guard-room and comes back with a bundle. "You'll need these. Too many people have seen you." He tosses me a filthy rag that turns out to be a woman's tunic. "And here." He adds another rag. "Cover your hair and part of your face with this."

Arthur accepts the scraps of clothing that Jon gives him and begins pulling them on.

Jon swipes his hand through the thick layer of soot behind the torch and rubs it into Arthur's hair. "You still look like one from the South." He reaches over to the bottom of the tunic I'm wearing and tears a strip off. "Try this." He binds the rag around Arthur's head and down across one eye. "That covers more of it. And stoop if you can. You're far too tall for a slave."

Arthur grins. I think he enjoys following Jon's orders. "And just what is your plan, Jon of Enfert?"

"You'll each carry a jar. Keep it on the shoulder closest to the crowd and look down at your feet all the time. If anyone asks for wine, say you'll be back directly with fresh—that your jar is empty."

"Do you have a way off this island?" Arthur asks.

"Two friends and I plan to take a boat at high tide. I've convinced them to take the two of you; they know Ilena, of course, and I said you were the Dragon Chief who might rid us of these Saxons if we could save you also."

"Good plan. And the only one that might succeed. You've worked with the boats before?"

"A bit," Jon says. "I hope we can row free of the tide on Clota and get into Leven."

"You'll have to," Arthur says. "East on Clota is all Saxon camps for as far as the tide goes."

One guard is sprawled across the table, his head resting beside a pair of knucklebones; the other lies curled up on a pile of straw. We step over the man on the floor and inch carefully around the one at the table.

Jon carries the torch, and Arthur lifts the jar to his shoulder. Wine slushes inside as he positions it, and he tilts the jar mouth upward. When we get outside, Jon points to another jar beside the door. "Ilena, carry that one. And both of you, listen well. We must separate; three together may attract notice. Can you find your way to the boats?"

"Straight down the path?" Arthur asks.

"Aye," Jon says. "Keep going down, and you'll get there. The jars go into a shed just beside the building where the guards stay. The boat will be at the end of the shed, but we'll only wait a few minutes. It is dangerous, and we must leave as the tide comes in to get safely away."

Arthur nods, and I heft the empty jar onto my shoulder. The three of us hurry along the path, and by the time I come out in front of the rectangular building, Jon is out of sight and Arthur is far ahead of me. I pause to look at the empty space in front of the bench and wonder where they've taken Durant's body—then I swallow hard and move on quickly.

The fires have died down to low mounds of glowing coals. Most people seem to have retreated into whatever shelter is provided on this crowded island, but here and there a small group lingers in the near-darkness. Occasional bundles on the ground mark folk who've fallen asleep outside.

I lose sight of Arthur's tall figure almost at once as I scurry along, close to the rock wall on my right, while keeping the jar on my left shoulder so that it hides my face.

No one stops me, but once I hear a man call, "Wine! Wine! Over here, woman!"

I do not hesitate, but slip into the deep shadows of the narrow descent with his curses following me. At the bottom the few sentries on guard barely glance at me as I rush by and turn into the shed. I put the jar down among others like it and follow Jon's directions to turn to my right as I leave the little building. A boat much like the one I saw on the lake floats below a flat rock ledge.

Nol, village leader of Enfert, and Fiona's husband, Craig, are side by side on the center plank seat.

Jon's voice is muted but urgent. "Get in. We can't take Arthur."

I've grasped the edge of the craft with one hand and am reaching for Jon's outstretched arm when I realize what he said. The boat is small, with only four seats. "He must get to the Ford of Leven," I say.

"There's no room," Jon says. "They couldn't get a larger boat."

"Then I'll stay here and you'll take him. I'll be right back with him."

"Ilena!"

I hesitate for only a moment. "No, Jon." I turn and run into the shed, where I grab an empty jar and lift it to my shoulder.

As I pass the sentries, one looks up and calls, "Still drinking up there, are they?"

"Aye," I say. "And in a hurry, too."

As soon as I'm out of sight of the guards, I set the jar down and race into the narrow passage as fast as I can, praying that I don't stumble on an unseen obstacle.

Arthur is easy to find. A group of people surrounds him and a heavyset warrior.

Arthur speaks in a surly voice. "I'll bring wine, sir, if you but let me go for it. This jar is empty."

"So you've said," the other says. "But when we called you over here, there was wine in it, and you poured for two others and then spilled what should have been mine."

"I'm sorry, sir. I did not see the piece of firewood that tripped me." Arthur points to the rag around his face. "I've been wounded and lost an eye."

"I wonder what an empty eye socket looks like." Firelight reflects off the blade of a dirk. "I'll take that rag off and look."

I pull some strands of hair out to fall around my cheeks, stoop to hide my face, and scream as loudly as I can, "So 'ere you are, Barra, you bloody fool. Lookin' all over an' you've been trouble enough already today." I push my way into the circle and grab Arthur's arm. "You'll come back wi' me now, you will. And no arguing about it. What you're doing nattering with folk when the jars have to be put away, I don't know." I pull him away from the man with the knife and drag him through the circle. A woman steps aside to let us pass, and others are chuckling at the display.

"And where's your jar, you worthless idiot?" I turn back to the circle to see if the man with the knife is following. He isn't; he stands openmouthed, watching us. "I'm sorry," I say.

" 'E's not right in the head sometimes and 'e forgets what 'e's supposed to be doing."

Arthur has bent to pick up his jar, and I grab his arm again. "Come along. We're late 'n' there's work to do before we can sleep. Hustle now."

We get to the narrow passage in a few quick steps, and once hidden from view in the darkness, I pause for a moment to be sure we weren't followed. The group we left seems to be enjoying a joke at the expense of the man with the knife.

"Well done, Ilena," Arthur says. "I couldn't take on all of them, and I was out of ideas."

"Everybody likes to watch someone get yelled at," I say. "We have to move fast. Jon can't wait long for us." I know better than to tell Arthur that I can't go too. There's no time for arguing.

We plunge down the passageway as fast as we can, stopping only for a moment at the bottom to retrieve my jar.

The sentries see us coming, and one calls out, "What's your hurry now? Don't tell me they want more wine."

"Oh, they do," I say. "But we're supposed to straighten the whole shed before we go to bed."

The sentry laughs. "Don't make too much noise. Everyone down here is sleeping but us, and we're ready for some quiet."

"Yes, sir," I say.

When we get inside the shed, Arthur and I set our jars down and race out the back door of the building. There is no boat.

"They've gone without us," I whisper. "They said they might."

"Psst! Ilena!" It's Jon. I look around but can't see anything except water and rock. "Up here. Take a few more steps and then climb up the rocks."

Arthur is ahead of me and reaches back to pull me up the steep layers of rock. The moon is giving enough light for me to make out Jon's figure in front of us.

"Now," Jon whispers, "down another set of rocks."

Arthur braces himself on Jon's shoulder and drops down into the darkness. I take Jon's arm and follow.

Craig and Nol already have oars in the water; Jon steps into the prow and keeps one hand on the rock to steady the boat.

I give Arthur a slight push. "Get in. Hurry!" I whisper.

He steps carefully into the leather shell, then turns toward me and says quietly, "But there isn't room for all of us."

At almost the same moment, Jon says, "I'll stay. At least I'm not marked for beheading."

I hesitate for only an instant while a picture of Kenna, large with their child, flashes through my mind. I bring my fist down hard on Jon's arm, and he releases his grip on the rock. I shove the boat away from the shore with my foot and watch the rising tide whirl it out into the current.

Jon falls backward onto the front seat, and he and Arthur both stare back at me as Nol and Craig fight the racing water to turn the boat into the mouth of River Leven. I watch the little craft until it disappears in the darkness.

Chapter 15

"Where are they?" It's one of the sentries. He must be standing on the ledge outside the wine shed. A cliff blocks my escape from this spot. The only path out is back over the rocks the way I came.

"I know she didn't come out the front door." This voice is getting closer; the man must be partway up the steps that lead to where I'm standing.

"Who are you looking for?" I call in as sullen a voice as I can manage.

"What are you doing? You're supposed to be in the shed. And where's the one with you?"

I pull myself up the rocks and stare straight at a sentry who has started up the other side. "What do you think I'm doing? Looking for a moment's privacy, that's what. There's no time up top to find the latrines and precious little time here. What's a person supposed to do?"

Both of them laugh and the one down on the ledge says, "All right. Come on over here where you belong. We're supposed to make sure no one gets off the fortress."

"And how would I manage that with all the water around it?" I grumble. When I've cleared the top of the rocks and moved down a couple of steps, I jump onto the sand below and stomp into the wine shed with them following me. I don't remember seeing either of them when the band from Dun Struan brought me in earlier tonight, but I still try to keep my face away from them.

"There was a tall man with you. Had a rag over his eye. Where's he now?"

I hope he's well upriver with the tide, but I say, "How should I know? Worthless clod. I left him here cleaning up. And he hasn't done it and there's a jar missing, so I've got to go up top looking for it. Will one of you give me a hand here? I'll be up till dawn getting this all done alone."

This brings a bigger laugh. "Sorry, dearie. It's your problem. Good luck in finding a wine jar in the mess of people we've got here tonight."

They leave me alone, and I sit down on a crate to think for a few minutes. I could never get past the sentries here to take the path that I came in on with Hana and the Dun Struan war band. Arthur mentioned a north entrance near the prison cell. If I can find it, perhaps it will lead to a way off the island.

I clank a couple of jugs around and move some crates so that it looks like I've done something, then saunter out of the storage shed and take the path that leads between the peaks. One of the sentries looks up from his spot near the fire, but doesn't say anything.

Once through the narrow passage, I walk around the edge of the flat area; no one is awake that I can see. I stop again near the place where Durant died. I feel like lying down on the spot and crying, but I clutch his ring through layers of fabric and remember how his arms felt around me.

The night before he left Dun Alyn, he said, "I will not always be beside you. A chief must be strong enough to stand alone when she has to."

I think of Spusscio and Belert watching me ride away from Dun Alyn, of Eogan waiting and worrying beside River Leven, and of Vorgel's faith in me. I take a deep breath and hurry into the shadows behind the building.

The prison is dark, so the guards' fire must have burned out. I have to find a way off the island before they discover that their prisoners are gone.

"Quiet at last." It's a man's voice and it comes from somewhere in the dark to the north of me.

"About time. And they'll be up early for the behead-ings." Another man, in about the same place.

"Likely. And the rest of the day getting ready to march on Cameliard. Glad I can stay here and guard the fortress."

"Aye, I've no desire to go off with a bunch of Saxons and fight Cameliard."

I can't see anything in the darkness except a faint glow from a small night fire. The north entrance would be guarded, so I suppose these are the sentries. I'm afraid to step out from my place against the cliff; there is enough light from the smoldering coals of fires behind me to make me visible.

"I'll be glad when that Dragon Chief is done away with tomorrow."

"He's got a charmed life for sure, but we have him safe now."

"Aye. No getting out of that prison."

"It's dark over there. Why'd they let their fire go down so far do you think?"

There's a silence and then a flash of light as one lights a torch.

They're headed this way!

I hold still and press myself against the cliff. Just as they come close enough to spot me, they veer off toward the prison.

Now is my chance. When the sentries enter the guardroom, I run as quickly as I can toward the spot that they have left. Just past their fire, a rocky path slopes into darkness;

I can hear shouts from the prison as I try to keep my balance on the rough terrain.

Most of the night has been overcast, but now the clouds part, and there is enough moonlight for me to see the path. A short distance ahead, the earth seems to drop away, and I check my speed just in time to see the track turn sharply to the right. If the moon had not appeared when it did, I'd have plunged over the cliff.

The noise above me is increasing, but I don't waste time worrying about it. The moon disappears again, so I slow to a careful walk, staying close to the rock face. There is a slight glow somewhere in front of me; I've been heading east, so I must be approaching the channel that we crossed.

The path descends, and I come out on the east side of the fortress, only a short distance above the beach. The large wooden boat that ferried us from the mainland is drawn up onto the shore, and a small leather currach lies upside down beside it.

The only people I can see are two sentries far to my right, where the path leads around to the south entrance. The flickering light from their distant fire helps me pick my way down steps in the rock to the beach, and the sand softens my footfalls as I flatten myself against the steep cliffs.

The water level in the channel is higher now than it was when we arrived. I do not know the currents here, but perhaps the high tide that carried Arthur to freedom is still rising. If it is, the stream before me will take me up into

River Leven; if the tide has turned, I will be swept down past the sentries, into River Clota, and past the guarded beach on the south of the fortress. There I'll be seen and captured again or else washed out into the western ocean.

There is a disturbance at the sentries' fire; two warriors, armed with spears and shields, have arrived. Their voices carry clearly above the sound of the river.

"The prisoners have escaped. Have you seen anyone?"

"Nothing here. When did they get away?"

"Don't know. The guards were sleeping."

"Wouldn't want to be them when Camilla hears."

"Keep an eye out. We think they were seen near the wine shed."

Soon everyone on the island will be searching; if I don't get away now, I will be found. I run, stooping as low as I can, to the shadow cast by the large boat. When I'm safely hidden against its rough wooden side, I sit still, listening.

"Look everywhere! That's orders."

"Well, you can see there's nothing out here."

"Right. You're to start in by the shed and search back to this spot. Then stay where you can see the channel. We're going to look around the prison and start checking everyone sleeping up there."

I have a little time while they're searching around the shed; I must get off the island and out of sight before they come back.

I crawl to the currach and lie flat on the sand while I

examine it. It's even smaller than the one Craig and Nol guided out into River Leven. There is an oar lying underneath, and I can feel a plank across the middle that must serve as its only seat. The shell is hardened leather, and wooden ribs inside provide stability and places to step.

The voices have faded. I crawl to a point where I can see around the prow of the wooden boat. There is no one at the fire now; all four of them are moving past the corner of the cliffs. Fear holds me immobile for a brief moment, but I force myself to risk everything on this fragile leather craft and the chance that the current in the channel is still running upstream with the tide.

I crouch down as far as possible and run to the water's edge, dragging the boat and oar along behind me. It takes three attempts before I'm safely seated and floating in the shallow water along the edge of the channel.

I give a hard push with the oar and shoot out into the current, bobbing along like a piece of driftwood. The tide is still rising, and my small craft turns north, heading upriver toward the Ford of Leven.

At first I'm so grateful to be safely away from the fortress that I don't mind what my stomach does as the boat spins and bounces on its way. However, when the stream joins the current that whirls around the north side of Alcluith, my speed increases, and the spinning becomes unbearable. My first attempts to steer with the oar nearly capsize the craft, but at last I manage a system of quick paddle dips that stop the spinning without threatening to dump me into the river.

The seat is well below the rim of the boat, and I keep my body bent so that I won't be seen from the shore. The boat might be mistaken—I hope—for a large log being washed in with the tide. Smoke and the dull glow of night fires mark the camps along the right-hand shore. The moon has set and I'd guess it to be only a short time before daylight.

Too soon the tidal current slows, so I paddle to increase the boat's speed. After some jerks and near-spills, I master the rhythm, but by then the tide has turned and the retreating seawater combined with the natural downstream sweep of river water is more than I can overcome. I try to move the boat toward the left shore, where I might find safety in the deep darkness—perhaps even locate Eogan and Machonna in our camp spot of last night—but one paddle stroke goes deeper than I intended and sends me toward the right-hand shore.

Before I can recover control, the leather boat scrapes to a halt on the river bottom, beside a brush-covered shoreline. I grasp a branch and pull myself onto the bank. At least I'm north of the enemy camps here, so I drag the boat up between two shrubs and sit beside it. I must be close to the ford, but I'm too tired to cross it and look for Eogan. I just want to get out of sight before it gets lighter.

The boat would be a clear sign to any pursuers, so I strip

off my boots and trousers, add the rest of my clothes to the pile, and wade out into the stream, dragging the boat, until the water is over my knees. I hold on to it for a moment, reluctant somehow to part with it, but then push it toward the center of the river and skim the oar after it.

"Good-bye," I whisper as I watch the downstream current take it and whisk it along until it is out of sight.

Before I return to shore, I dip down into the water and scrub as much of the filth and blood off my face and body as I can. I dry off with a few handfuls of leaves and pull on my clothes, tossing the filthy tunic and rag under a shrub, then pick up my boots and move closer to a large oak tree. I lean against the trunk and look up through layers of green leaves to the dawn sky.

The earth feels cool and solid beneath my bare feet.

Across the river I can see the hill I climbed at twilight; Eogan and Machonna must be asleep in the little glen on the far side. Arthur is somewhere nearby, I hope, and my friends from Enfert should be well up into the long lake by now. I smile at the thought of their homecoming.

The night seems a dream; so much happened so fast. Still, I know that it is not a dream, because Durant is gone. I look up to the sky, too weary and sorrowful to think, and let the pain flow through me and out into the air.

At last I tug on my boots, then push through underbrush to the path and set a brisk pace northward. By the time I pass the ford, the sun is rising; I continue for a short distance, then veer off the trail and up into tree cover, where I break off pine boughs for a bed. Despite the thoughts that come as soon as I'm still, I am so exhausted that I fall asleep within moments.

Chapter 16

I dream of Durant and see again the sword that Sorcha drove into his body; I dream of Sorcha in my weapons class as we practiced the grips a warrior uses to slice or stab or parry. And I dream of fear and cold.

Then I feel soft warmth against my body. I hear horses nearby—and voices, getting closer.

"Up here!" Eogan is shouting. "It's Ilena!"

"Tell Arthur." Spusscio's voice. "The dog found her."

My eyes snap open, and I turn toward the warmth. Machonna lies beside me with his muzzle near my head; he aims a hearty lick at my face.

Eogan, managing to look angry and relieved at the same

time, stands over me with Gillis and Spusscio close behind him. "You were supposed to come back last night."

Pine boughs scatter as I scramble to my feet.

Vorgel pushes past Eogan to embrace me. "We feared for you. I am so relieved that you are safe." She holds me firmly, and her eyes are moist. "Arthur is angry that you tricked him, and Eogan is cross with all of us for letting you go into danger."

"Arthur knows why I tricked him, and Eogan must learn that I am a warrior." I speak firmly, but I stay close to Vorgel and keep looking from Spusscio to Gillis and on to Eogan to be sure that they are really here with me. Machonna's body presses against my knee, and I keep a hand on his rough head. The fear and despair that haunted me through the night begin to drain away.

Spusscio sounds as cross as Eogan looks. "You were to find a brave deed to do and come back to us—not disappear completely for over a month and get yourself into a prison on Alcluith."

Vorgel speaks before I can defend myself. "She has done what I would expect of the daughter of Cara and Belert. She rescued Arthur at considerable danger to herself and, as I described to you, put her own desires aside to help her people in the Vale of Enfert." She turns to Gillis and waits for him to speak.

His voice is as deep and stern as I remember it. "There is

no doubt that Ilena has fulfilled the conditions for her return as chief of Dun Alyn." He pauses and looks at me solemnly. "The way of the warrior is difficult. Bravery is required, but so is kindness; skill with weapons is necessary, but so is patience with others; the warmth to attract followers, but also the strength to act alone; the heart to grieve and the soul to feel joy in life."

While Gillis is speaking, Arthur comes into the clearing. He says, "And few there are with all of those gifts, Gillis. Dun Alyn is fortunate to have Ilena."

I am too overcome by their words to answer. Vorgel puts her arm through mine, and we walk out of the clearing together.

The others are waiting on the trail. Arno looks uncomfortable on a gray mare; Hoel and four warriors whom I don't know are talking quietly together while their horses crop grass nearby.

As I prepare to mount Rol, Arthur comes to my side. "Durant told me that you have more courage than most," he says. "He was right." He looks up at the sun, midway in its arc to noon. "My head would be looking at the sky from a spearpoint now if you hadn't come to my rescue."

"It was Jon," I say. "He rescued you."

"It was not Jon who came back into the fortress and snatched me out of danger. And it was not Jon who pushed me into the boat and shoved it out into the current."

There is a jingle of harness and a creak of leather as the

rest mount and begin moving north on the trail. Arthur looks at me in silence for a moment, then says, "I won't forget your loyalty, Ilena." He turns to go toward his horse, then stops and looks back at me. "How did you get off of Alcluith?"

"You mentioned a north entrance," I say. "Just as I found it, the sentries went to see why the prison was dark, and I slipped down the path. When I got to the beach along the channel, there was a small leather boat. It seemed the only way."

"Thank the gods you succeeded." He hurries to his horse and mounts.

The trail is wide enough here for two horses, and Vorgel falls into place beside me. We ride in silence for a time, then she says, "Arthur told us about Durant."

I remain silent. I cannot forget the sight of his body facedown on Alcluith with Sorcha's sword protruding from his back.

She continues. "His death is a terrible loss to Arthur and to Britain." She sighs. "There are no words of comfort that I can offer you." She reaches over and clasps my hand. "Only that life goes on, Ilena. It does not seem so now, but it does. Gradually, slowly, happiness will creep back into your days. Welcome each bit that appears, because it will mean that you are healing."

I put my other hand over hers. "I can't feel anything but despair," I say. I let the tears fall, and we ride together until the trail narrows, then I slow Rol to allow her to move ahead of me. As I follow her, I can see the slump of her shoulders and her occasional attempts to ease her position in the saddle. I wonder how old Vorgel is and marvel at her stamina; she has traveled steadily for at least eight days and goes to a battle that will determine the fate of Northern Britain.

We push on as fast as we can through the afternoon and evening and make our night camp near a deserted tower of the ancient ones. We are in Cameliard's territory now, and we should arrive at their mustering field early in the morning. I lie down with Machonna at my feet while the others are still talking around the night fire.

When I awaken, dawn has stained the sky a brilliant rose color, and the horses are ready. Eogan hands me my waterskin. "I've filled it for you, and Machonna has had a drink from the stream and bread and meat for breakfast."

We are on our way as soon as we can see the trail. It keeps to high ground to avoid the marshes that stretch across the plains beside us, and we soon have a good view down the valley to the cliffs of Cameliard.

All my life I've heard of the famous fortress set here at the eastern entrance to the North, but the tall gray cliffs with the meadows before them, the river looping behind, and the rampart walls rising above are a picture far more dramatic than anything the bards could portray.

Our path winds around the side of a rocky hill and comes out at the wide plain below the fortress. The entire area, including the meadow and the slopes of the surrounding hills, is filled with war bands that spread in a thick circle around a central field. In the open space, chariots race and pause so that a chief or Druid can speak to the troops, then race again, making a brilliant pattern as harness fittings, trumpets, sword hilts, and burnished helmets catch the morning sun.

When we stop to look over the scene, Gillis is beside me. "There," he says. He points at a spot in front of the cliffs. The black banner with a white goshawk in the center waves above Dun Alyn's troops. "Your father will be happy to see you; he has spent the days that you've been gone grieving and worrying about you."

I long to see him, too, and I turn to see if Arthur is ready to move on. One of his warriors is unfurling the red and white dragon banner. Eogan is nearby, and his face shines with the excitement of riding onto the field under Arthur's banner.

"Ilena." Arthur motions me to him.

"Hoel will ride at my shield side as usual," he says. "You know that Durant rode on my sword side?"

I nod. The greatest honor a warrior can have is to ride at his chief's sword side. That was my place beside Belert at the Ford of Dee.

Arthur continues. "Will you ride at my sword side today?"

He watches me as I realize what he said. "I'd be pleased," he adds, "if you would take Durant's place."

I finally find my voice. "I'm . . . I'm honored!" I say.

And so, with the dragon banner fluttering over us, I ride at Arthur's right hand down onto the mustering field and hear the noise diminish to silence as war band after war band recognizes the Dragon Chief.

Author's Note

When I read the literature that has come down to us through the oral tradition—that is, the folktales, myths, and legends of olden times, with their mix of facts and fantasy—I find myself trying to imagine a reality behind the stories. How did people actually live? What did they wear, eat, drink? What were the houses like? And what true events lie behind the exaggerations, superstitions, and magic?

We can never know for certain. The old stories come from a time before written language and have been told for so long that their origins are lost. The first descriptions of events and people in Britain were written by the Roman historians who accompanied Julius Caesar in 55–54 BC.

The Romans came back to stay in AD 43, and life for

Britons in the occupied area—what is now England—changed greatly. The Romans were unable to conquer the North—what is now Scotland—so life there continued much as it had for centuries.

When the Romans left Britain around AD 400, Germanic tribes from Europe began invading. The Saxons were one of the first groups to come, and the British, without Roman protection and with their own structures of government and war bands weakened or gone, had trouble defending their land. By AD 500 Saxons and other invaders controlled most of southeast Britain.

It was around this time that a strong resistance movement arose somewhere in the vicinity of what is now the Scottish-English border. Many experts believe that Arthur was the leader of an alliance of tribes that held back the invaders for nearly forty years.

The stories about Arthur that are most familiar to us were written by Chrétien de Troyes, who lived in France in the late 1100s, and Sir Thomas Malory of England, who wrote around 1470. These authors set their stories in their own times, and in them Arthur is a king and his war band is made up of knights of the late Middle Ages. However, the real Arthur and his followers would not have had suits of armor, large horses, stirrups, squires, fancy palaces, elegant clothing, elaborate banquets, or any of the other trappings of the High Middle Ages.

Another difference between these romantic stories written about Arthur and the reality of life in the Dark Ages was in the role of women. In the North of Britain women were warriors, chiefs, Druids, and—most important, perhaps—heiresses to land and fortresses. One indication of the widespread participation of women in war bands is that Adomnan, abbot of Iona (a monastery in what is now western Scotland), felt it necessary to make a law in AD 697 ordering that women not go into battle. Adomnan's Law was enforced from time to time, but it was many years before women disappeared completely from war bands throughout the North.

Much of what we know about the sixth century in Britain comes from archaeological discoveries. Pottery shards and remnants of rectangular Saxon houses indicate that Saxon expansion halted during the first half of the 500s. Archaeologists have discovered evidence of round structures built by the native Britons—some as large as ninety feet across that probably served as Great Halls, and many smaller ones in which families lived. The defensive rings of earth and occasional thorn hedges that surrounded fortresses in the old stories have been verified by archaeological digs. Excavations have yielded jewelry, scraps of clothing, tools, weapons, and utensils from the era.

In my quest for a realistic setting for my fictional heroine, I've visited many of the locations described in *Lady Ilena: Way of the Warrior*.

I spent a wonderful afternoon exploring spectacular

Dunnottar Castle on the northeast coast of Scotland—right where I imagined Dun Alyn to be. While my companions poked around the remnants of fifteenth-century buildings on the site, I tried to visualize the fortress as it would have been in Ilena's time. I looked out on the North Sea and down to rocks at the bottom of the cliffs just as she would have. I pictured round thatched-roof buildings and the bustle of life inside the compound, as well as small farms and settlements in the surrounding fields.

At Dumbarton Castle—called Alcluith in the sixth century—we drove onto the castle grounds because the channel that had separated the fortress from the mainland is gone now. I climbed up behind a seventeenth-century building, through the narrow passageway where Ilena is startled by Jon's presence, and out into the courtyard where she stands before Faolan and Sorcha. I climbed to the very top and looked across the river Leven toward the hill where Ilena surveys the nighttime scene before she is captured. I studied the sheer cliffs below me and imagined that the channel to the east was still flowing between fortress and mainland. I could picture the difficulty Ilena would have in getting away from this place.

At Stirling—Cameliard in the sixth century—I stood at the ramparts atop the high cliffs and stared down at the plain below, where the final scene of *Lady Ilena: Way of the Warrior* takes place. I could almost see the banners, the chariots wheeling about the field, and the sun glinting off gold sword hilts and harness fittings. The wind whistled around me, and I wished that the city noise would stop so I could listen for trumpet blasts and the shouts of the Druids as they roused the fighting spirit of the war bands. I looked to the southwest, hoping to see Ilena, Hoel, and Arthur leading their little band down onto the battleground, but of course they were not there.

My search for answers to my own questions has led to this book, and I hope that my writing helps readers, as it has helped me, see the Dark Ages more clearly.

About the Author

Patricia Malone grew up on a farm in central Illinois. She is a former teacher who has traveled extensively throughout Great Britain, researching its history, legends, and folktales. She is particularly interested in Scotland, the land of her ancestors.

Patricia Malone lives in Naperville, Illinois. Her first novel was *The Legend of Lady Ilena*.